KU-229-149

Deep Pocket

'This is the start of a series that will feature Inspector Henry
Peckover, tough minded, tough fisted, not at all averse to
bending the law a little (or a lot) if it will help him get his
villains. Henry has a long-suffering mistress, a Cockney
accent and an ability to write poetry that is published in
the most intellectual of journals. It's a quirky combination,
and Kenyon makes the most of it as he sets Henry off in
rapid and dogged pursuit of the team of big businessmen,
Arab tycoon, and bent police officer and his seductive wife,
all of whom are deep into fraud and financial skulduggery.
Not even a command to drop the case from high up in
Scotland Yard stops our man, and the climax, during a
country grouse shoot, is indeed a shoot-'em-up humdinger.'

Publishers Weekly

'Murder and wit, humour and action, all are nicely com-
bined.'

Oxford Times

'A trail of violence and gripping action spiced with absurdity
and wit.'

Bolton Evening News

'Peckover is truly an original, and I look forward to meeting
up with him again in the not too distant future.'

Dublin Sunday Press

Deep Pocket

Michael Kenyon

MAGNUM BOOKS

Methuen Paperbacks Ltd

A Magnum Book

DEEP POCKET

ISBN 0 417 03300 1

First published in Great Britain 1978
by William Collins Sons & Co. Ltd
Magnum edition published 1979

Copyright © 1978 by Michael Kenyon

Magnum Books are published
by Methuen Paperbacks Ltd
11 New Fetter Lane, London EC4P 4EE

Made and printed in Great Britain
by Richard Clay (The Chaucer Press) Ltd
Bungay, Suffolk

*This book is sold subject to the condition that it shall not, by
way of trade or otherwise, be lent, resold, hired out, or
otherwise circulated without the publisher's prior consent in
any form of binding or cover other than that in which it is
published and without a similar condition including this
condition being imposed on the subsequent purchaser.*

CHAPTER I

For the fourteenth consecutive June day the heat enclosed London as with a band of steel, vibrating in the streets and squares, parching the parks, putting a song in the hearts of the vendors of overpriced ice-cream at Marble Arch and Charing Cross, and confusing the half-million tourists who had flown in on the airlines of the world with a certain knowledge of only two facts of British life: that their money would buy them anything, in which they were roughly correct, and that here was the metropolis of perpetual fog. A BBC voice on the one o'clock news was first with the awaited announcement of a ban on hosepipes for watering gardens and washing cars. In a fountain in Trafalgar Square two travellers from Sydney stripped, banged beer cans and were led away by the police. From Heathrow and the main line railway stations decanting the cross-channel hordes the foreign flood gushed in. In the shopping thoroughfares the only British citizens to be seen were the bus conductors from Jamaica and Pakistan, their double-decked buses budging with the massed traffic in ten-yard bursts at three miles per hour. Areas of the West End looked like *The Desert Song*. The pavements of Oxford Street were filled with Arabs. Arabs, French, Dutch, Germans, South Americans and Orientals filled the Marks and Spencer's, elbowing and carousing among the cashmere and denim. Japanese and Arabs filled the X-certificate cinemas and looked sideways into the windows of the porn bookshops of Soho. Americans filled the stalls at the National Theatre.

A smell of decomposition and the naked body of a very young call-girl, Dawn de Nuit, filled most of the floor space of a fourth-floor room at the Georgian Hotel, Rydal Street, Bayswater.

In his fifth-floor office at New Scotland Yard, Detective-Inspector Henry Peckover of the fraud squad received the news by telephone. An internal call. Sergeant Windle, records.

'Sir? Should interest you. We've a dead tart in Bayswater. Hotel in Rydal Street – the Georgian. North end of Rydal Street, Paddington really. Bashed to blazes.'

Inspector Peckover's head flipped back. His mouth was agape in relief and he was ready to cry, 'Wrong customer, laddie! Up yours!' He leaned forward, composing himself.

'Sorry, sonny, you're out of date. I'm fraud.' The vowels were not markedly mangled but Professor Higgins would have placed them. Henry Peckover had grown up in Poplar. 'I've been reshuffled. Since Monday. I'm the logarithms and Swiss bank accounts now. Got a calculator – we've all got calculators up 'ere. Thanks anyway.'

'There's a whisper one of her clients might have been Zadiq. He's in your Molehill file.'

'Ah.'

Peckover eyed the Molehill file open on the desk beneath his nose. Or to be precise, part one of the six-part Molehill file was open. Parts two, three, four and six were in the desk beneath his dozen copies of the *Listener*, freshly-bought, and judging by the progress he was making they were likely to stay in the drawer. Part five seemed to be missing, fortunately. No one appeared concerned, the only response to his queries about its absence being, 'It's the reshuffle, it'll turn up.'

Pity parts one, two, three, four and six had not been mislaid in the reshuffle as well. Four days in fraud after six years in vice and he'd done nothing but gaze in wonderment at copies of balance sheets, minutes of meetings, letters to planning sub-committees and memoranda from finance joint-committees starting, 'Reference yrs of the 9th inst SPC/FIN/0401/818T/78 . . .' The file was not headed the Molehill file either, it was headed Greenmead (South Bushey) Development, East Middlesex Borough Council (Greater London AY2/2/1FS), Blue Confidential, Dept. C6/7. One of the villains was supposed to be a builder named Mountain, in fact two Mountains, father and son, of whom a frustrated predecessor in fraud had remarked that there was no breaking of Mountains out of this molehill. The name Molehill had stuck, like a code-name for D-day but without expectation of success. Cover and contents alike were to Inspector Peckover a mystery, indecipherable and charming, like hiero-glyphics on a new-found Rosetta Stone. Each day for four broiling days, the new boy, he gazed into the file with a wild surmise and a sense that he as well might be looking into Chapman's Homer, translated back into the Greek.

But the name Zadiq was therein. Frequently. Without Zadiq, so far as Peckover had been able to discover, there would have been only half a Greenmead develop-ment. All the private stuff, the split-level housing estate, the hotel, the proposed link road from the estate to the M40, all that as distinct from the ratepayers' contribution – new council offices, shopping precinct, comprehensive school, high-rise flats – all that private bit was Zadiq. Or Zadiq and his Gulf Consortium. Zadiq had already bought up many of the better carpeted corners of central London. Now he was moving out into the green belt. Sheikh Mohammed Zadiq had oil money cascading out of his ears.

'Zadiq, eh?'

'Georgian Hotel, sir, Rydal Street. The heavies are there. Be like old times for you.'

'Where d'you hear about Zadiq?'

'In fraud, sir. I was reshuffled too.'

'It's like a whist drive. D'you 'ave anything on 'im?'

'Less than you've got in the Molehill file, I'd say. I'll send up what there is.'

'What about the girl? Whaddyer say 'er name was?'

'Dawn de Nuit. Bashed with a television set. Could've been the repair man. They're a sullen lot, my experience.'

'What repair man's that?' Peckover stretched out a hand for the Molehill file.

'Hypothesis, sir. Sorry. An idle remark, you might say. Hello? Sir?'

'Very idle and comic. I'm 'olding my sides.' Peckover pulled at his lower lip. 'Dawn de Nuit.'

'Thought you might've come across her in vice, sir.'

'What's 'er real name?'

'Possibly Ann Evans. There's a widow woman on the same floor says there were sometimes letters for an Ann Evans. Only Ann Evans we've got here tried to poison her husband in Walthamstow, nineteen forty-four. Killed by a flying-bomb. If she were alive she'd be a hundred and six.'

Ann Evans. Peckover cogitated, his free hand now plucking at his ear. He had reached his mid overweight forties. His cropped hair had turned grey above the ears and the grey was daily spreading. When he cogitated his hands went into action, pulling at earlobes, stroking his nose, scratching his scalp. He had never wanted to be a policeman. His father had been a policeman and he, Henry, eldest of nine, had found himself insinuated into the force. He still did not want to be a policeman but whatever chances there might have been for a change he had let slip by. How else after a quarter of a century at it could he earn a living? Security at Selfridges, watching for the shoplifters, on his feet all day, bored silly?

'Don't know any Ann Evans. I'll 'ave Terry Sutton take a look. And where the offence is, let the great axe fall.'

Silence filtered through the telephone. Peckover replaced it, looked round the office and recalled that Detective-Sergeant Sutton, reshuffled with him from vice into fraud and supposed to be his right hand, was in Croydon sleuthing after the source of nine hundred forged credit cards.

At least the air-conditioning functioned. That was more than could be said of the Scotland Yard of yesteryear, on the Embankment, fifteen years back. At the desk by the window sat Sands, the civilian accountant, pursuing figures through a ledger with covers which were veined like a gorgonzola. Into a telephone at the corner desk pensionable Milton wheezed and cackled to his mother. Harris, eyes ringed in grey like an unrinsed bath, a vacuum flask beside his typewriter, peeled an apple. Others toiled in adjacent offices but here was Peckover's section, and Sands, Milton and Harris, unshuffled for an appearance of continuity, had all denied responsibility for the Molehill file. To send any of these to Rydal Street would be to risk rioting – or worse, another reshuffle. The comic in records might be reshuffled back. Detective-Inspector Peckover picked up his telephone and asked for an outside line. He dialled the catering manager at the Royal Archaeological Society.

'Miriam?'

'Henry?'

'What's the menu tonight?'

'Aubergines.'

'Again?'

'Should be plenty of moussaka. They'll go for the salmon. They never touch the moussaka.'

'Why d'you give it them?'

'Why d'you think?'

'Be careful.' The warning was mechanical. Peckover had been issuing the same warning to his fiancée since the start of time. One day the bottom of Miriam's basket would give way as she headed out of the marbled vestibule of the Royal Archaeological Society and there'd be doggy-bags of moussaka, onion soup and profiteroles bursting over the polished boots of the doorman. 'See you around six or seven.'

'Heard that one before. I'll keep it warm.'

'This is different, love, I've told you. Office hours. I'm a clerk. Quill pen and ready reckoner, six and twelve make eighteen, carry the one. Look, buy yourself today's *Listener*.'

'Henry – it isn't!'

'Best reading in town. If they've sold out, don't worry. I've got a couple of extra copies.'

'Henry, that's marvellous! Did you know? I mean, didn't they write and say yes? I'm going straight out – '

'Can't stop. 'Bye, love.'

He put on his jacket, slipped into the inner pocket a folded *Listener* for reading on the Underground and told Sands he was going to Rydal Street.

He took the Circle Line from St James's Park. In a corner he unfolded the *Listener* and turned the pages, tense as an Olympic finalist coiled for the gun.

Bang. There he was. A sandwiched half column, with Dostoevsky, Symbolism and Sensitivity on the left-hand page, and on the right considerable drivel about The Media and the Moral Equation. His own effort held them apart.

SUMMER SALE

'May his soul rot a seed a day in hell.'
Those un-Reformed monastics, clerics, dons
Knew how to damn. Goodbye to that. The Mons
Retreat with candle, book and bell
Regained a little of what reason smashed.
Hands up whose fathers found at Mons a creed
More potent than these drums at Austin Reed
Sale of the Year – Buy Now – All Prices Slashed –
Men's Oaths and Summer Oathing –

'This please the train for going Ealing Broadway, sir?'

He was Persian, or Guatemalan, wedged and puffing in the adjacent seat, his head angled into an eyeball-to-eyeball position with Peckover. He nursed a briefcase stuffed with dinars. Madagascan, Peckover decided. The policeman inhaled rare spices.

'Ealing Broadway. Yes. That's to say, no. You're all right. Change at Earl's Court. Get the District Line. Dis-trict Line.'

Walking through waves of heat from Bayswater Tube station, Peckover passed the Jolly Gardeners, saloon bar door hooked open to reveal a tempting dark interior. He resisted. The Georgian Hotel in Rydal Street was Victorian and terraced. At the door stood two helmeted constables, shirtsleeves rolled up to the elbow, and on the pavement the press and a scatter of locals. A grizzled pressman with jungle eyebrows and a camera lifted a hand in greeting.

'Morning, Mr Peckover. Hear you've a poem in the *New Statesman.*'

'*Listener.* If it changes your life you can buy me a beer.'

'Thought you'd transferred to fraud,' said the *Express* crime man in the polka-dotted bow-tie.

'Just passing.'

He passed by the press and into the hotel, flicking open his wallet with his warrant card at the nearest constable. A third constable stood apart from a huddle of guests and staff by the reception desk. He came forward and Peckover showed the warrant card. There was no lift. Peckover made for the stairs, followed by the eyes of the huddle.

The carpet was threadbare, the walls pock-marked as if unsteady furniture removers had been at work. An inadequate 40-watt bulb lit the fourth-floor passage. Advancing along the passage, straightening his peaked cap, came Chief Superintendent Farnsworth. Peckover swallowed a groan. Farnsworth – Himmler of the Yard.

Not Himmler, more Goebbels, Peckover thought. Did
he mean Ribbentrop? The propaganda and public
relations man. Farnsworth, late of the fraud squad, had
been promoted in rank to a new post, Co-ordinator
(Metropolitan Area), Community Relations. Which
meant race relations. Which would mean, come another
couple of years, if the mayhem between police and blacks
were reduced, and even if it weren't, an OBE for Farnsworth. Possibly a knighthood. Walking, the gap narrowing, Peckover reflected that nothing would be less likely
to improve race relations in the streets of North Kensing-
ton and Brixton, or more likely to bring on new nights of
whirling bicycle chains and broken heads, than Farnsworth.

'Last door on your right, Henry,' Farnsworth said need-
lessly. A fourth constable and a man changing the film in
a camera stood outside the last door on the right. In the
passage hung a hint of a cheese smell. 'Wild-goose chasing
after Mr Zadiq?'

'There's word he might've been a customer.'

'Well, words are your forte, Henry. Understand you
have another rhyme in the public prints. I'll read it, I
will indeed, if you send it along some time. Tell me, have
you considered a pseudonym?'

'What's wrong with Henry Peckover?'

'Nothing, nothing wrong with it. Goodness, our sensitive scribblers. But quite apart from your position in the
force, one or two doubts I've heard voiced at the top –
commissioner level, Henry, between you and me – well,
it's hardly poetic, not precisely a poetic name, wouldn't
you agree?'

'None of the young ones are these days. They're all
Jack 'Arbottle and Mavis Clamp.'

'Precisely. The young ones. Think about it.'

Peckover tilted his head and raised his eyebrows at the
desiccated arsehole-creeper in his new silver pips and

braid and rimless spectacles like a sadistic schoolmaster's in a German film of the thirties. Unjust that the Co-ordinator (Metropolitan Area), Community Relations, should have a height advantage of six or seven inches.

'Yourself, sir – didn't think I'd find you 'ere. 'Ardly a racial thing this one, is it? Case of once a fraud man, always a fraud man?'

'Not a bit of it. You may not be aware but there was trouble this way two nights ago. Kingston Klub in Westland Terrace.'

'Didn't see anything in the papers.'

'Precisely. What my job's about, Henry. The media have agreed to play it down. I've a lunch conference with the television news directors at twelve-thirty.' He re-straightened his cap. 'All three channels.'

All three, Peckover mused in admiration, watching the receding blue back of Farnsworth. Lunch too. After the sherry and Campari sodas. The cheese smell became a smell of silage and drains, thickening as he continued along the passage.

There was a sitting-room of sorts, ill-furnished and shabby, with the window open and traffic noises rising from the street below. A detective-constable he knew by sight was on hands and knees with a metal measuring tape, muttering measurements. Another detective was jotting them in a notebook.

Detective-Inspector Kenneth Long, flying squad, looked up from the notebook and said, 'Tennyson himself. Goin' to write a sonnet about her, Henry? "Earth hath not anything to show more fair"?'

'Stuff it or I'll shut the window.'

'Bedroom's through there and good luck. If you can tell me whether she was fair, dark or Caribbean blue, I'd appreciate it.'

There was no telling. In the bedroom Peckover looked down at Dawn de Nuit. Flies circled above what had been her head. The television, a battery-operated colour portable, was also beyond repair. By the look of it, and of Dawn de Nuit, either the set had been dropped on her or flung down on her. An unmade double-bed and a dressing-table occupied most of the room. On a chair were a skirt, panties and white blouse. The window was wide open but to no great effect. Peckover backed out.

'When?' he said.

'Night before last,' Long said. His skin had turned not brown from the sun but lobster. The raw face glistened either with a skin cream or sweat. 'Or early yesterday morning. The doc was here. Said he'd phone.'

Peckover regarded the telephone on the chain-store table. Dawn de Nuit, call-girl. Did she receive calls from Kuwait? 'Stand by, Dawn de Nuit. Sheikh Zadiq is arriving nine-hundred hours at Heathrow. Flight BA-stroke-one-two-three . . .' Also on the table were a transistor radio, a pop music magazine, a nasal inhaler, paper from a chocolate bar and a half-filled ashtray.

'Who found 'er?'

'Smelled her. There was a complaint, bloke in the flat down the passage. It's not refrigeration weather. Being starkers doesn't mean she was working either, not in this heat. What're you here for, Henry?' Long had moved to the open window. He put his head out, inhaled dust and petrol fumes, retrieved his head. 'We had Farnsworth five minutes ago looking for blackies under the bed. Fraud a bit quiet for you?'

'One minute I'm told this girl services a Mr Zadiq, next Farnsworth says I'm on a wild-goose chase.'

'You're interested in Zadiq?'

'Dunno. Early days.' He was not interested. He wanted to sit in a pub and write a poem. ''E's the one bought the Regent Tower and didn't get Claridges or the Berkeley. 'E's killing time with this Greenmead development where there was all the bedlam over the green belt, writs flying

for libel and defamation and they sacked the planning
officer because 'e kept saying the whole council was
pocketing bundles of twenties from a builder called
Mountain, and Mountain was pocketing every contract
from motorways to the public lavatories, and the MP was
always in the south of France, and our sheikh flashing 'is
teeth, and whither democracy, O Lord, and 'ow long will
thy ratepayers smart under the rod of the corrupt, O
Zion, and thy servant in fraud under a load of old
balance sheets?'

'Nine foot six door to door,' the constable said, and
released the tape. It snaked back into its case with a
metallic rustling.

'Stick with the heavies, Ken,' Peckover said. 'Fraud's
like Alice in Wonderland, like being sucked into a tunnel
where it's raining digits. There's no saying the source of
sudden prosperity for a few on the Greenmead picnic is
Zadiq but the loot's come from somewhere.' He joined
Long at the window, gulped Paddington fumes and dust.
'That fat alderman, Beeston, remember, in and out of the
gossip columns with his Mercedes and telly starlets. The
MP's an anonymous twerp, except he's double-barrelled,
Ames-Clegg, and 'e's got four 'ouses. Farnsworth chased
it for two years and got nowhere. Only geezer who ever
seemed to be getting anywhere was that Aussie reporter
on the *East Middlesex Advertiser*, Carter or Cartwright or
someone, and 'e was sacked. Beaten up too, person or
persons unknown, only 'e refused to file a complaint. And
the planning officer, Malcolm York, 'e was sacked – and
got a letter saying 'e'd be done, same as the reporter, if 'e
didn't belt up. It's all politics. The council, the MP, right
up to the 'Ome Office. The council as Tory as afternoon
tea and the 'Ome Secretary pocketing 'is twenties, I
wouldn't wonder. Fraud's where they send you when
you're not quick enough to say no. Least, the Molehill file
is. Now we've a dead tart who might or might not 'ave

jiggled the sheikh's ding-dong and what's that got to do with anything?'

'Let me know if you find out.' Long, catching the constable's eye, pointed at the ashtray. 'If Zadiq used her it'd hardly have been here. Try the Regent Tower. Better still, don't bother. Zadiq flew to New York on Saturday. He's been gone five days.'

'Great.' Peckover watched the constable slide the ashtray and its contents into a plastic bag. 'Thanks. Fraud squad inspector, freshly translated, in pursuit of wild goose. What else?'

'Nothing. She might've been an Ann Evans.'

'I 'eard. What about the telly repairs man?'

'Who?'

'Never mind. If you're holding back you'll get sod all from me on the telly repairs man.'

'Looked like she lived here, mean it's not just a working pad. Clothes, winter boots, woolly hat, all the gear. She took the flat on – ' Long consulted the notebook – 'second of April. It's flats from this floor up, the hotel's below. No handbag, letters, papers, insurance card. Nothing.'

'Removed by the man from the telly repairs.'

'Who's this bloke from the telly repairs?'

'You should look into it. What else? I've this laughable feeling you're not sharing.'

Long was patting his creamy red cheeks as if consoling them for dire experiences. 'Found a watch.'

'Made in Abu Dhabi?'

'Made in Japan.'

Peckover opened the labelled plastic bag and took out a watch, holding it by the edges of its chain strap. A Seiko, not obviously new, stopped at six thirty-three. An oil sheikh, he considered, might have been expected to wear a Patek Philippe. Possibly. He turned the watch over.

Engraved on the silver case in a copperplate flourish was the dedication, *BB. With Admiration.* 8. 12. 1975.

'Inspirations?' Long said.

'Brigitte Bardot,' said Peckover.

'It's a man's watch.'

'I can see that.' He returned the watch to the bag. 'She might 'ave manly wrists. Play your cards right, there's a trip to Paris in it.'

'If you don't mind, why don't you go and uncover a fraud?'

'Course, if you'd rather, there's the slog round the engravers of the western world and the weekend with the birth certificates at Somerset House. Can't be more than a couple of thousand BBs with birthdays on December the eighth.'

To avoid the press Peckover left the Georgian Hotel by the kitchen. He nodded with courtesy as he passed a youth in an apron, weeping over onions on a chopping-board. In the Jolly Gardeners he carried his pint to the telephone.

'Sutton? Good lad. Where the 'ell 've you been? Don't tell me. Listen, if you can bear to drop the credit cards for a minute, take a fast look in the Molehill file, first folder, top left-hand drawer. Or it might be on the desk. Give me the birthday of Alderman Basil Beeston. 'E's in the dramatis personae bit early on.'

The beer was cloudy, thin and life-saving. Peckover, waiting, burped and sighed. Why, he wondered, did policemen have to pretend to be so cynical and hard, like adolescents? Fifteen minutes he'd spent with two heavy mob men and that mess which had been a girl. Three policemen if you counted Farnsworth and not a word of pity for the girl from anyone. No emotion. Cold concrete. To be realistic, Peckover considered, swallowing beer, she may well not have been a fun-loving, healthy and lovely girl with her life ahead of her. She may well have been a tough, unhealthy and lovely girl with her life ahead of her.

'Yes? . . . February fifth, nineteen-eighteen. Pity. Listen, go through the file and check for anyone with a birthday on August twelfth . . . Who? Grouse shooting begins? Grouse-shooting begins what? . . . Grouse shooting begins on August twelfth?'

Peckover glowered. Among the myriad names and numbers scribbled on the wall above the telephone he read, 'Check up on your doctor, he may have VD.'

'Look, lad, I'm giving you this number and you're phoning back in one minute to tell me what East Middlesex Council's doing this afternoon. Are they doing anything or are they in recess and if they are when do they fling themselves into action? One minute, lad. Or I'll 'ave you reshuffled into stores and equipment.'

CHAPTER II

'Only point I'd add, with respect,' Alderman Basil Beeston said, 'is that if all the tripe talked by our Marxist friend could be cooked and vinegared and carried to Wembley we'd have had enough to feed the Manchester United lot last month.'

'Hear hear!'

'With leftovers!'

'Except, I submit, there's tripe and there's tripe and the quality of the tripe we're accustomed to being served by Mrs Isaacs I'd not give to Corporal, who for the information of Mrs Isaacs is my golden retriever. A pedigree specimen, let me add, in fairness, with more brains than the communists and foreigners on this council can show between them. The brains of our pinko friends would have to be served with microscopes, garnished with quotations from their flabby führer, Herr Marx – '

Beaming amid renewed uproar of applause, laughter and isolated savage booing, Beeston sat. The councillor on his right, rocking with merriment, placed a hand on Beeston's shoulder as if to steady himself. On Beeston's left a woman in a floral hat stared straight ahead, neither applauding nor booing but smiling like a winner at the annual chrysanthemum competition. A rumpled figure sitting alone at a central desk among papers and books banged a gavel without conviction.

Town clerk? wondered the man peering down from the public gallery. Chairman? Bailiff? Lord-Lieutenant of the East Middlesex Marches?

' – characteristic racial smears of Alderman Beeston, who is the real führer here – '

A small intense woman was on her feet, black hair coiled in a chignon, voice carrying high above the hubbub. Mrs Isaacs, the man in the public gallery advised himself. Forward the revolution, Mrs Isaacs.

' – been regaled often enough about the matchless Corporal whenever the motion concerns school meals, the rates increase, Greenmead, anything at all of consequence to our tortured ratepayers – '

'Tortured – ho!'

'Wake us when it's over!'

'Make it a single, Betty, it's too hot for the long-player!'

' – dog of such breeding should be named Corporal, not Field-Marshal, passes comprehension unless its master can't stomach a second Field-Marshal in competition with himself. And for the information of Field-Marshal Beeston we know far too much about the noble Corporal, by now everything there is to be known except of course his source, whether he came in a package deal with the Mercedes from a certain building contractor who must remain nameless, or whether – '

'Withdraw!' cried a voice from the benches under the arched nineteenth-century windows.

' – or whether he was a bonus following Field-Marshal Beeston's holiday last October at the Europa Hotel in Torremolinos, or the two weeks at the Madrid Hilton – '

'Withdraw!'

'Old stuff, Betty!'

'Take her out in the street – where she came from!'

' – or whether he was part of a separate deal over the contract for the Greenmead swimming baths which went as usual to our nameless builder friend in return for such favours conferred as the motor cruiser now moored at Lymington, I believe, and the house, number six, at Oaks Avenue – '

'Shame!'

'Sick commie psycho!'

'Gentlemen – ladies – !'

East Middlesex Council was on its feet. Mrs Betty Isaacs stayed on hers, her mouth inaudibly working through the tumult, one arm raised like a prophet foretelling doom. The rumpled lieutenant at the central desk passed a hand across his brow and in the process of banging his gavel let it slip from his fingers to clatter along the tiled floor of the gangway. An ageing councillor had climbed on a bench and was screaming vituperation at Councillor Isaacs. Alderman Beeston, arms folded and legs crossed, smiled.

Above unseemliness, he waited, surveying the spectators in the public gallery. They were as few as usual with the one exception. The three pensioners who had come in from their seat at the corner of Queen Street; the nun and party of sixth formers from the Mary Magdalene Convent; Mrs Oates, twice-defeated Labour candidate for the Camberley Ward; and apart, at tables roped off from the public benches, the press, two of them, the North London stringer hoping for a tenner for a paragraph in

the London evenings, and the girl from the *Advertiser*, both
bored and talking to each other, too experienced to heed
the unprintable slanders cannoning round the chamber
beneath them. The stranger in the gallery sat hunched
forward, chin in hands, observing. Observing for most of
the time Basil Beeston, it seemed to Beeston. If the Greenmead enquiries hadn't petered out months ago and he
hadn't had it on good authority they were unlikely to be
reopened, he'd have said the man was a copper.

No thanks to the rumpled lieutenant, groping across
the tiles after his gavel, the frenzy subsided to a rumbling.
Portraits of departed worthies, starched and whiskered,
leered from the walls of the Victorian council chamber.
Draughts air-conditioned the chamber, swirling round
the feet of the members and freshening the gallery. A
motion was proposed seeking government aid for convert-
ing the gravel pits at Bell Lane into a recreation centre. A
man with a raffish air and an eyepatch who looked like
Colonel Dayan argued that with the West End fifteen
minutes south-east and the green belt five minutes north-
west, money for a recreation centre was money down the
plug. Alderman Beeston pointed out that under Section E
of the Local Government Land Reclamation and Pre-
servation Act (1976) the raising of the matter at borough
level was out of order. The recreation centre was referred
back to committee, agreement was reached on post-
poning the next full session from October third to October
tenth, and the meeting was adjourned.

Alderman Beeston swallowed a whisky and water in
the mayor's robing room which next year would be his
own robing room. Alderman Basil Beeston, Mayor. First
thing he'd do would be bloody sure he had a new set of
robes, not the gipsy rags Reg and a half century of pre-
decessors had hung on themselves for the ceremonial
stuff, stained with tea and mucus and brown sherry.

'Thing about Rimini is going to be all that pasta and

muck,' Beeston said, swirling the whisky in a pudgy hand.

'Travel broadens the belly,' said Alderman Wicks.

'Mr Beeston, sir?' A porter in a black tie stood in the doorway. 'There's a gentleman asking for a word. I've put 'im in the waiting-room. An Inspector Peckover, sir.'

'Peckover? Bloody traffic department. They got me coming off the M1, Saturday night.' He finished the whisky. Fifty-eight and jowly with high blood-pressure, he was aware he should have been drinking cocoa. 'Wait, I'll come with you.'

In the corridor, walking, Beeston told the porter, 'Haven't time for this speeding rubbish now, Arthur. Here's what you do. Give him five minutes, then you sprint in and tell him you couldn't find me, I'd gone. All right?'

He slid a five-pound note into Arthur's hand, patted his shoulder and took the left turn which led past the documents room and the treasurer's office and through the side door to the car park.

At home he sought out the housekeeper to discover if there had been messages, bathed, packed, checked his contraceptives and air ticket to Rimini, then settled down in the lounge with whisky and *Penthouse*. Corporal arranged himself for sleep at his feet. In the corner cabinet stood Toby jugs and miniature liqueurs; atop the colour television, a gilt Zulu, poised for assegai-throwing.

Beeston poured a gigantic tot. Almost as good as the jaunt itself, he considered, any jaunt, were these last waiting hours. Martha happy and absent, conducting the Women's Institute round the tea rooms of Devon; the boys at their toffee-nosed boarding school, arrogant brats writing letters which began *Dear Mother and Father* and ended *Yours Sincerely*, but both well and not at home.

'Whaaar,' he wheezed, turning a *Penthouse* page and

surveying the ripe melons of the bum of Dawn Woodhouse, 20, sales clerk of Kimberley Terrace, Coventry. You could almost see the goose pimples.

The level in the whisky bottle had sunk by a quarter when he heard the doorbell ring. Corporal hurtled from the lounge. Beeston waited. Corporal returned with Mrs Sullivan who said, 'There's an Inspector Peckover asking after you.'

'Say what he wanted?'

'He did not.'

'Did you tell him I was in?'

'I said I'd look.'

'Motoring rubbish.' Beeston stood up. 'I'll not be pestered. Would you tell him there's no one here, I've gone, I'm on my way to Rimini. Wait, no. Just tell him I went to the airport. You could mention Gatwick. Say there was a cab here. Could you manage that?'

'Why could I not? It's the car drivers are hounded from here to the grave. Will I say 'tis a business trip?'

'No, no. Don't elaborate. It's all the truth, near enough. I'm leaving right away.'

He watched by the window of the spare bedroom until the policeman had walked back to his Ford Cortina and driven away. In his own bedroom, he telephoned for a radio cab to Heathrow. There'd be four hours waiting and he'd have to keep an eye out for this Peckover but there was no taking it easy here any longer. He dialled another number and asked for Willie McLeod.

'Not 'ere,' a voice croaked. 'Dogs innit? Dogs night. Catford. Wotcher want?'

'Nothing. Not important. Goodbye.'

Three hundred miles north, beyond green belt, industrial belt, peaks and dales, more industrial belt, more dales and upon empty moors which knew nothing of drought, the rain bucketed down. The London policeman, parked where he saw between the other parked cars only a white gate and a corner of imitation wall, switched on the windscreen wipers. A sodden figure in a black jacket and riding hat galloped from the direction of the marquee and out of sight beyond cars.

'. . . hope we'll be able to carry on with the last two events but you'll agree it's not too promising,' drawled a voice over the loudspeakers. 'Just to confirm the results of the dressage, first was Sir Cyril Ames-Clegg on Patchwork, eighty-nine points. Second, Miss Charlotte Bentley . . .'

Five minutes earlier the sky had been blue. The policeman had found a sign pointing to the Committee Tent, a promising enough place to start. Then the sky had darkened, opened, and everyone had charged for cover. Now he sheltered in the borrowed car. He might have been parked on the ocean bed. The ocean had begun to enter the car and unless the deluge eased there was going to be one defunct policeman, drowned at Hexham Horse Show in this leafy depression on the Northumbria moors. The car had been loaned grudgingly by the Newcastle Constabulary, and while it looked to be in reasonable nick, somewhere above the driver's seat or where the door was supposed to fit, or the window, the rain came in, seeping at first, then spattering, now in a flurry of hot globules which detonated against his face and completed the soaking of his right side from shoulder to shoe. They'd done it deliberately, he was certain. Sodding Geordies. A leaky car and local knowledge of the impending downpour.

The car to his left reversed through the mire. Other cars were leaving, one towing a horsebox. A lake had formed beneath the white gate. '. . . extremely disappointing . . . most unlikely we're going to be able to continue . . .' the voice crackled. A drenched figure in jodhpurs and riding hat ran with a horse from behind the competitors' tent.

The car to the policeman's right reversed on slithering tyres.

He turned off the windscreen wipers and opened the car door. If he didn't move he was going to be left as the last survivor of the Hexham Horse Show. A wall of rain drove him back into the car.

At least he'd seen Hadrian's Wall, a mile away, if it had been Hadrian's Wall. Glimpsed it switchbacking over the moors when the sky had been blue. Shifting his weight in the driver's seat and listening to the squelching sound, Peckover reflected on rheumatism. One cheering aspect was that Ames-Clegg and the horse crowd would be as wet.

He reflected on horses, cavalry, Hadrian's Wall. He took out a ballpoint pen and wrote minutely along the edges of his programme, expunging and inserting, muttering, closing his eyes and pulling his earlobe:

'Apres le deluge, moi,' a soldier said
In prophecy, recruited from his bed
At Colombey-les-deux-Eglises to man
The cerulean wall which Hadrian,
Imperator, built in an idle hour
For Lady Hadrian, dishonoured flower
Of Rome, cheated while cheating with her knaves
Of consuls, senators and household slaves.
This soldier, Darius, or Jean-Pierre,
A Gaul, raw-knuckled legionnaire
Press-ganged with fifteen thousand able oafs
From Gallia, Germania –

Pigswill, thought the policeman, looking through the windscreen. He blinked. The rain had eased to a drizzle. Two men in raincoats were prising a white gate from the mud; a woman trotted a horse across the grass. But where was everyone else? Where the cars, the idiot voice over the loudspeakers? He cursed, screwed the programme into a ball and climbed from the car. Where that horrible MP?

Sir Cyril was soaping, scrubbing and singing airs from *Glamorous Night* in the mosaic and marble master bathroom of his Georgian house on the other side of Hexham. He was on the underside of sixty, winner of the dressage for the fourth consecutive year, and apart from a recurrent stomach disorder, in the pink. Pinkly steaming he came into the bedroom.

'Do hurry,' Millie Ames-Clegg said from her perch at the dressing-table. 'You know how prompt Jack always is.'

'By the old Moulmein pagoda looking lazy to the sea,' boomed Sir Cyril, questing for underwear in the fitted cupboard.

Jack and Dorothy Newby, he counted, and the Hugh-Percys, and Binkie, and the Hugh-Percys' cousin Edith — or Elsie, was it? — whom he had never met, a lady-in-waiting to the Queen. He'd better have Elsie or Edith on his right.

In the drawing-room, humming, he checked the cigars. The grandfather clock chimed. Davis came in and said, 'Excuse me, sir, there's a policeman, an Inspector Peckover.'

'Eh?'

'From London, sir. He said if you could spare him a moment he'd be grateful. An informal matter, he said.'

'Informal matter about what?' Sir Cyril said loudly.

'He didn't say, sir. I could show him into the library, sir, or the boot room if you prefer. He's very wet.'

'Wet, is he? Show him the gate, Davis, the gate! We've company, does he realize that? I'm not having policemen banging about my house when there's company! Wet or dry!'

'I'll inform him, sir.'

Sir Cyril started to recount the cigars but he was upset and at fourteen or fifteen he lost count. He stalked to the library and looked across the back lawns to the kitchen door but saw no one. Great Scott, was the fellow at the front door? Rain sluiced down. Davis stepped into the library.

'Pardon me, sir. He's very adamant. He says he'll try to be brief and it will be simpler in the long run.'

'Simpler?' Sir Cyril shouted. 'Adamant? If he wants to see me he can communicate with my secretary at the House – arrange an appointment in the normal way! What d'ye say his name was?'

'Peckover, sir.'

'Peckover! Tell him I'll remember Peckover! We still have some rights to privacy in this country, Davis – what? Tell him I'll peck him over! Go on, man! I'll peck him over, you tell him that!'

Mollified by this last shaft, chuckling almost, and baffling the lady-in-waiting on his right by chuckling aloud more than once while he sipped and picked through the tomato soup, beef with mashed potatoes, and brown bread pudding, Sir Cyril discovered he had forgotten the policeman's name.

Was it the name he'd make the joke about? What name? What had the joke been? Whatever the name, the blighter'd been sent packing.

Hangover? Bendover? Picklock?

He'd ask Davis some time. Davis would know.

'There's a copper been asking for you, Mr Mountain. Audrey was on the blower, said I should pass it on and could you ring 'er about the steel? Peckover, 'is name was. 'E was round the office before lunch.'

'Which office? Baker Street?'

''S'right. Wanted to know where 'e could find you.'

'What's he want?'

'Audrey said 'e wouldn't say. Only where could 'e get you?'

'Get you in the goolies, that's where they get you, give 'em a chance.'

Thomas Mountain, chairman and managing director of Thomas Mountain & Son Ltd, lifted his white helmet and mopped a bald, sunburned head. He looked like a baked potato, mopping and advancing over timber, skirting a cement-mixer, heading towards the foreman's hut. Beyond the hut a crane was unloading concrete blocks. A bulldozer shunted rubble. The sun spilled upon labourers stripped to the waist. But progress had been delayed by a steel shortage and Mountain was in ill humour.

He was seventy and the best years were yet to come, the most prosperous years. Business expanding, three new offices opened since Easter in the midlands and the north, the corruption alarms evaporated. But the steel was a devil. He'd shoot 'em, trade unions, government, the lot. Now the coppers again. Were the alarms going to start all over? Had they got something new? Flanking Thomas Mountain, a pace behind, eunuchs attending the sultan, walked the site foreman and Rupert, the chairman's son and deputy chairman, both in white helmets.

In the foreman's hut Thomas Mountain rapped a hairy knuckle on an architect's drawing. 'We'll start on the pipes – here. Tell the men I'm paying time and a half for every forty yards dug by the weekend.'

'Time and a half's steep, Dad. They'll do forty yards – '

'Time and a half for every forty yards and if you've nothing else to do you could try taking off your coat and finding a shovel.'

Rupert Mountain regarded his father's round shoulders, hunched over the drawings. There were times he could almost have put a knife in them.

Peckover, brooded the father. Peckover? What else

could it be but Greenmead again? They didn't go snooping to your head office for a parking offence or not paying
your telly licence.

'Guv?' A youth with tattooed butterflies on his forearms stood in the open door of the hut. 'Copper askin' for
you. Peckover or somethin'.'

The silence in the foreman's hut continued. The youth
opened his mouth to speak again.

'Where – here?' Thomas Mountain said.

The youth looked across the wasteland of the building
site and pointed. 'Talkin' to Charlie.'

The squarish distant figure with Charlie was two or
three minutes walk away.

'You tell him I was here?'

'Didn't know, guv, did I? Didn't know where you
were.'

Mountain handed the foreman car keys and said, 'You
haven't seen me. Tell Eric to bring the car round to the
back gate.'

Mopping and grunting, glancing over his shoulder to
make sure he was keeping the hut between himself and
the policeman, Thomas Mountain strode out. Rupert
Mountain scampered to keep pace.

'You can't hide from the police. It's crazy.'

'Shut up. I'm not starting over again with all that
business.'

'You're not going to stop it by clearing out.'

'You want to stay and have a cup of tea with him, you
stay. How'd we know it's not you he wants? Been rough-
ing up one of your tarts, have you?'

Rupert Mountain said nothing and the father showed
no interest in answers. By the time they had reached the
back gate the Rover was waiting. They threw their
helmets on to the back seat. Rupert drove.

'Stop at a telephone-box,' said the father. 'Have you got
Willie McLeod's number?'

'For God's sake, you're not going to put the boot in! Not a copper!'

'Who's putting the boot in? Wet behind the ears, you are.' Thomas Mountain stared through the window at the redbrick terraces of north-west London. 'Just some spadework, an enquiry or two.'

'Buy him, Dad. God's sake, we don't want Willie McLeod. Anyway, Willie wouldn't, bet you. Not a copper.'

Buy, always buy, brooded Thomas Mountain, thumbing through his son's address book. He was sick to the teeth with buying. Buy, buy, buy.

If someone had to be bought, the Willie McLeods came cheaper than coppers, usually.

'You're right,' Thomas Mountain said. 'Still, I'd like to know a bit more about him if I've got to see him. Peckover, is it? There's a phone box – pull over.'

CHAPTER III

Thunder rumbled over London but brought no rain. The drought persisted. The second drought in three years. On *This Week* a climatologist forecast that the earth's climate was returning to the drought, famine and political unrest of the neoboreal era. On 1 July the temperature at Kew reached 94 degrees.

By confining himself at the Yard instead of careering through city, suburbs and furthest countryside Peckover had accomplished by the second week of July the impossible: the reading of parts one, two, three and four of the Molehill file. Part five had not yet turned up. Part six he brought home and positioned by the sofa with a pint glass and two bottles of beer while he plumped the cushions and unlaced his shoes. He picked up the file,

emptied his mind of distractions, then stretched out,
barefoot and ready for hypnosis.

Reading the Molehill file was not the same as under-
standing it. Many of the pages, Peckover believed, might
have sold well as a cure for insomnia. Certainly they could
mean nothing to anyone except a genius accountant. But
letters and memoranda which had passed between
Alderman Beeston, faceless officials, council lawyers and
the sacked planning officer, taken in conjunction with the
balance sheets, did suggest something smelly had been
going on. The £16,000 cheque from East Middlesex
Council to Thomas Mountain & Son for 'costs, machinery
and material invoices M49–M63 in excess January price
index' coinciding, for example, with the delivery date on
the Mercedes 210 sold by Horne Garages to Alderman
Beeston. Smell being heaped upon smell by the additional
revelation that Alan Horne, director of Horne Garages,
was a brother-in-law of Rupert Mountain. None of which
proved anything. All was smell and suggestion with too
many references to inflation as the cause of expenditure
above original estimates. The clippings from the *East
Middlesex Advertiser*, most of them by the sacked and
bludgeoned reporter, Carter, sketched in a racy background of council overspending and favouritism in the
awarding of contracts but shied away from naming names
and concentrated on mild, probably heavily-edited in-
nuendo. Part six of the file, mercifully thin, brought the
affair more or less up to date.

Peckover read, dozed and drank beer. Through the
open kitchen door percolated a gamey perfume of long-
hung pigeon or partridge or something shot.

He had not exerted himself since the cocked snook
from three of the file's leading dramatis personae. Hadn't
he done his bit in vice, knocked himself out? Now, in
fraud, pride in work seemed to have flown out of the
window and lassitude come in. Or a sense of proportion.

Why cripple himself with ulcers and cardiac arrest when merely by going through the motions he'd probably achieve as much? That day by Hadrian's Wall, he might have caught pneumonia. The actuarial tables didn't show many coppers waltzing into their seventies. Coppers, bus conductors, dentists. He was no longer a sprig and if he were to try his hand at a full-length verse play now seemed the time. Perhaps the powers at the Yard had guessed at the change of life creeping over him before he had known it himself. Perhaps fraud was where they put you to graze when policeman's lethargy struck.

Swallowing beer, muttering when a rivulet coursed down his chin, Peckover realized he had discovered a new affection for home. The sitting-room of the house in Islington was over-furnished with an accumulation of his own and Miriam's inherited bits and pieces: three tables, too many table lamps, armchairs, chests and commodes, a chipped upright piano on which Miriam played halting Scarlatti sonatas, wastepaper baskets, clashing paintings of harlequins and Venetian canals, a tin filing cabinet of poems, rejection slips and tax papers, a threadbare Persian carpet, bookcases, all battered and amiable. The winey, gamey stew aroma sidled in from the kitchen. It was all a change from the six years of evenings extending into nights and mornings among pimps, porn, drugs and raids on the Chinese gambling parlours of Gerrard Street.

Or it might have been but for the unresolved link be-tween dead Dawn de Nuit and Mr Zadiq, currently understood to be in Zurich. Ken Long's last report on Dawn de Nuit, sullenly passed on after three requests, threw little light on Dawn de Nuit, Zadiq or anyone else. She had indeed been Ann Evans, 18, hairdressing assistant from Abergavenny and on the game in London for the past six months. Murdered by television. A friendless girl apparently, apart from clients, who seemed to have been plentiful. Easy enough, Peckover knew, for an Aber-

gavenny girl to stay friendless in London for her first six
months unless she joined the Abergavenny Association
(London Branch) or pretended rugby fever and turned
up at London–Welsh social evenings. Long's appended
interviews with two score discovered clients – not so far
including Mr Zadiq – established no outstanding suspect.
How many undiscovered clients had there been?

He had a contact or two himself among the girls. He'd
look them up some time. When the weather cooled and
they wouldn't be quite so shiny with sweat and scent. Not
that it wouldn't rankle, doing Long's work for him.

His foot had gone to sleep. He shook it and read,
'. . . only the granting of a major interest in a building or
its site by the builder is zero-rated, similar grants by other
persons being exempt under Group 1 of the Exemption
Schedule. The Council would therefore draw attention
to item 1 whereby they, the members of the partnership,
not the trustees, provided the benefit of the consideration
accrues to the members of the partnership, are treated as
the persons granting the major interest in the building
(Notice No. 708).'

God in heaven.

'Miriam?' he called out. 'Bring me a small bottle of
beer, love.'

'Aren't any,' Miriam called back from the kitchen.

'Bloody are. By the dresser.'

'They're not small, they're flagons, they'll make you fat.
I've got some Beaune.'

'Bones're for dogs,' Peckover called and waited for the
groan.

Even a groan was not warranted.

They ate hare stewed with onions and herbs in white
wine and brandy and served with a mustard and cream
sauce and boiled potatoes. Peckover refrained from asking
where the hare came from. Or the other ingredients. The
raspberry shortcake bore, he could have sworn, the

thumbprints of archaeologists who had tested it before abandoning it. Miriam, dieting again, abandoned it too. They had been engaged for eleven years and living together for thirteen. Neither quite understood why they had not yet married but both believed the other understood and that the reason was to do with tax.

'Think I might walk this lot off,' Peckover said.

'Thought it was office hours these days.'

'Can't get 'im in office hours. 'E's either at the BBC or lunching in the VIP bit at 'Eathrow watching the immigrants. I'll be back about ten, eleven.'

'Where's he live?'

'Clapham.'

'How d'you know he's not watching the immigrants?'

'Done my 'omework. Come along, I'll only be ten minutes with 'im.'

'Thanks, I'm watching the box. There's a comedy series, honestly you should see it, witless, vulgar, they don't even know their lines. I'm hooked. Why don't you telephone?'

'Got to watch the whites of 'is eyes. If 'e misunderstands 'e's going to be very upset.'

'You're going to drink beer and remember old times.'

'In that case I'm not going.'

'You are, we need the expenses. You realize we haven't paid either the gas or the rates yet?'

He drove to the City, over Southwark Bridge and through the Elephant and Castle. The evening was as clear as if it were noon. Ice-lolly wrappings and scorecards littered the roads leading from the Oval. The flannelled fools of Surrey had been wielding the willow, he supposed. Beating the lights he spurted into Clapham Road. One success of his life had been avoiding involvement in cricket.

On the Common were dogs, couples, a trio throwing a frisbee, a fair which either had just closed or was about to

open, and youths, white and coloured, kicking an un-
seasonal football. Peckover felt the expected misgivings
over bearding the chief superintendent at his home. Not
really the thing. What if he were entertaining the
Director-General of the BBC? He had never visited 76
Clapham Avenue South and he braked, considering a
U-turn and not visiting tonight either.

Farnsworth's house was an Edwardian semi-detached
with a front garden as formal as its owner: a patch of
brown lawn, a herbaceous border and six rose trees lined
up like blood donors. Mrs Farnsworth opened the door
and said, 'Yes? Goodness, aren't you Henry Peckover?
The poet?'

Having met her at social functions once or twice, Peckover wondered why she had not made a stronger im-
pression. Fortyish, he estimated, not at all bad-looking, a
little dishevelled possibly, but lissom, even a shade
sensuous, either because the top buttons of her blouse were
adrift or her black slacks were size, well, whatever size a
slip of a teenager might have slipped into. The mouth
looked peculiar. There was something else but he was not
sure what. An enthusiasm, a vibrancy?

The vibrant enthusiasm with which she recognized
Peckover the Poet?

He would have liked to have reciprocated, greeted her
by her first name. Esmé? Una? She stood aside, holding
the door.

'Come in, goodness, what a treat! I take the *Listener*.
And I saw one in – was it *Punch*? Oh, quite a while ago.
Terribly sorry, have some Ali Izmir.'

'Who?'

'Turkish Delight.'

She proferred the cylindrical box in her hand. What
was peculiar about Mrs Farnsworth's mouth, Peckover
realized, was that it was full, presumably with Ali Izmir
Turkish Delight.

'Thanks, I won't.'

'Gerry!'

She called into the house and closed the door behind the visitor. Gerry? marvelled Peckover. The Stalin of Clapham Avenue South – Gerry? Gerry was for Saturday evening speedway riders.

'Gerry, it's – ' Mrs Farnsworth's hand rose to her lips. She leaned close. 'Goodness, is it chief inspector or superintendent – ?'

Peckover smelled gin. Gin and Ali Azmir. He'd drink gin too if he were married to Farnsworth. Hit the Ali Izmir too.

'Henry, heavens! Hello. What is it?'

'Nothing, really, just passing. Been in Croydon. Stopped by on the off chance. Matter of fact been trying to catch you at the Yard but it'll keep. If you're busy.'

'Very tied up as it happens. Speech at the Cambridge Union tomorrow. The commissioner recommended I accept, put the facts. Immigration. Anglia are televising it live.'

The chief superintendent wore an unnecessary silk dressing-gown, unless he were going to or coming from bed. The speech-writing dressing-gown, Peckover supposed.

'Quite an occasion, I'd say,' Farnsworth said. 'But never too tied up for a colleague. Olive, a scotch for the inspector – would you?'

'No, no, thanks all the same. I'll only be a moment.'

'Precisely. All the same. The scotch, Olive. No water – neat, isn't it, Henry? I'll have a cup of tea if there's one going.'

A grandfather clock which did not look quite right against jazzy contemporary wallpaper dominated the hall. Peckover followed down carpeted stairs to the chief superintendent's study. He assumed it was a study. There was a desk but no easy chair apart from the padded rocking contraption at the desk, and insufficient books and papers. On a shelf leaned a half acre of mirror; for admiring himself in his dressing-gown, Peckover assumed.

He lowered himself on to a chair as comfortable as the north face of the Eiger.

'This Molehill file, sir, part five – '

'Still missing? I'd heard from Inspector Veal. Between you and me, it's a trifle embarrassing. I wasn't the last to handle it but who's going to convince the DC I'm not partly responsible – if it gets as far as the DC?' He cast a cryptic look across the desk. 'And Henry, you can drop the "sir". We're not at the Yard.'

'When you left fraud on the Friday, ah – ' Peckover hesitated, rejecting 'sir and' 'Chief' and 'Co-ordinator'. What did he call the fellow? Surely not Gerry – 'that was the nineteenth, that whole cabinet with the Molehill stuff and all the rest of section three was shifted down to C-Six. Then on Saturday evening the inspiration from the deputy commander and on Sunday it all gets shifted up again. Both moves were by the two duty clerks, Tate and Jackson. I've seen them and I'd not like to swear either gives a monkey's for the Molehill file or 'as ever 'eard of it.'

'I talked with them too. I gave the keys to Sergeant Drake and he locked them in his desk until Monday, eight o'clock, when he handed them over to you. Meanwhile there were half-a-dozen civilians moving C-Six up to the fourth, and the night shift, and eight or nine from fraud and the whole of the weekend traffic section.'

'About four 'undred who could've 'ad access, given a quiet couple of minutes and an 'airpin.'

'Precisely. Internal enquiry?'

'No question. It's getting on for a month. Not that any enquiry's going to achieve anything but a file's been nicked. Mean, if the whole of Molehill were gone, all right. Next year it might turn up in forensic or the kitchen or a bucket at the back of transport. But just the one folder.'

'Precisely.'

'Mean, you never took part five –' Casual, old son, this is it, Peckover warned himself. Keep the whites of your eyes white, you're not interrogating – 'out of the office. Or any of them. Brought them here, f'rinstance.'

'Often. Signed them out and back.' Farnsworth gave a fulsome wave, showing off the study like a house agent. 'Only place I can get any work done, half the time.'

'I can see. Perfect peace.'

Olive Farnsworth had arrived and placed tea in front of her husband. Now she was twisting the cap off the whisky bottle. The blouse button had been buttoned and her hair brushed. Peckover detected scent.

'Steady, Olive, you'll have our inspector driving into a tree.'

'Yes, please – that's to say, far too generous.' Bless you, Mrs Farnsworth. 'Let me tip 'alf of it back.'

'Perhaps some water, Olive, for Mr Peckover?'

'Warm, cold or mineral?' Mrs Farnsworth said, smiling and departing up the stairs.

Farnsworth was frowning. Peckover watched until the chief superintendent's eyes lowered through rimless glasses towards his tea, then he took a strengthening swig from the tumbler, reducing the level by half.

He said, 'Could you give me an idea what was in part five? If it never shows up I'm going to be rather stuck.'

'One and two are largely the Greenmead background and Mountain – the council contracts. Three's Zadiq and the private sector, four to six are chronological. Five would've been the last quarter of last year, roughly. Some correspondence between the council and Zadiq – he put in three bids then, all successful. More Beeston and Mountain stuff. Nothing spectacular.'

'Ames-Clegg?'

'Don't recall. You know all the renovations to his Hexham place were by Northumbria Construction, a Mountain subsidiary?'

'Did part five include the names of the shareholders when Mountain's went public?'

'Might have, if they're nowhere else. The father and son own fifty-one per cent.'

'Anything more on that planning officer – York?'

'York's one big frost, all passion and politics and never a fact you could bring in evidence.' Farnsworth stirred tea. 'Henry, two years of it I had. They're tricksters, crafty as they come, and nothing to hang on any of them. Between you and me I'd not be surprised if the file weren't about to be shelved. Waste of manpower, officer of your talents. What about the MP – seen him yet?' The chief superintendent's lips twitched above the teacup in what might have been a smirk. 'Understand you had a damp afternoon at a horse show.'

'I'm allowed an appointment at the 'Ouse of Commons for October. This coming October, I think, but could be October next year.' Peckover regarded the still copious amber in his tumbler. In good time he would sort out Sir Cyril Arse-Clogg. If he could stir himself. 'Beeston's back from Rimini, might look 'im up. The Mountains, they're around. Just a question of stealing up when they're not looking. It was this missing file that was confusing.'

'Precisely.' Farnsworth's eyes roved to the unfinished speech on his desk. 'Any progress on the prostitute, the one in Rydal Street?'

'Ken Long plays it close and Zadiq's in Switzerland. 'Er bag and papers, they're still missing.'

Like part five, Peckover thought. Farnsworth's frown was now fully directed towards his speech. Peckover swallowed the whisky and stood up.

'Much obliged, really very grateful, quite a help.' Gerry. 'Must be getting home.'

In flowing dressing-gown the speech-writer ushered his
visitor up the stairs and through the hall. From hi-fi
equipment beyond a closed door boomed Wagner. Ought
to say good night to Olive, thought Peckover.

If the thought had occurred to Farnsworth he kept it
to himself. As he opened the front door a grinding of
machinery somewhere in the hall sounded through the
Wagner. The grinding became a metallic whirring of
spindles and ratchets. Peckover flinched, ready to duck.
Then the grandfather clock chimed twice. The time was
ten-fifteen. On the doorstep the policemen smiled and
nodded to each other. Peckover hiccuped.

Clapham Common lay in deepening shadow. Warmed
by whisky, inhaling the parched Common smell as he
walked along the empty pavement to his car, Peckover
noticed a man reading a newspaper in the driving-seat of
a Jaguar parked on the opposite side of Clapham Avenue
South. Like the Yankee cops-and-robbers rubbish on the
box, he thought; rubbish which he admitted only to
Miriam, who needed no telling, that he was partial to.

Grey saloon. HLM 559N.

He drove back towards the river, wondering if a poem
were welling. A beginning had happened but until
morning he'd not be sure if it were a poem or doggerel.

> This wasp that flounders in the wine
> Is cooked, from lack of interest.
> His lethargy is also mine.
> The red which laps his football vest
> Reflects the sinking in the west
> Of our shared concubine
> The sun –

Shared concubine? Bloody 'ell! And where else, mate,
would the sun sink? One for the wastebasket. Poems which
welled out of a quintuple whisky preceded by beer and

Beaune were suspect.

Peckover drove north along Clapham Road. He'd have to have a beer soon to dilute the whisky but he could have it in the company of a contact or two, if he could raise any before the pubs shut. He'd phone Miriam, tell her it might be midnight and there'd be an extra couple of quid expenses towards the rates. He certainly couldn't go straight home. What if that comedy series were still blazing away, the one where they didn't know their lines?

Only when circumnavigating the Elephant and Castle did it occur to Peckover that the evening had grown far too dark for the character in HLM 559N to have been reading the newspaper.

He looked in the driving mirror. All that was following was a 91 bus.

CHAPTER IV

'Look, I'm busy, don't mess about, wotcher fink I am?'

'You nice girl. I like.'

'Illgnung hrr haa.'

'Whassee say?'

'He say he like too ver' much. He like blonde.'

'Oh. Yur. Well, tolja, it's fifty pahnd for two hours. Each. Fif-tee. Two-o-o hour.' Ignoring the stare of the septuagenarian with the Guinness, his bony shank and hip cramped against hers, though that was not entirely his fault, not in this scrum, she spread the five fingers of one hand and the index and middle finger of the other. 'If y'aven't got it, wou'ja move off? Scarper. There's no room.'

Nothing was truer. The Intrepid Fox bulged with the outpourings of the cinemas and theatres, with moguls and aspiring moguls from the adjacent cinema industry offices, with itinerants, locals and the merely thirsty. For fifteen minutes Mandy had sat amid din at the miniscule table with the uncleared glasses and heaped ashtray. For fourteen of those minutes the two Japanese had sat with her, back to back sharing the one chair, polite but bargaining. Did they think she was a bazaar? They sipped ginger beer and were slung with cameras, even at this hour. Probably hoping to snap her in her birthday suit.

She'd have none of it. No bargaining, no pictures. They were like that, the Japs, clean and considerate, sweet in a way, but mean. P'raps it was cheaper in the East, all those opium dens and rickshaws.

'Ng haa gnung owlish haa whah.'

'Whassat?'

'He say twenny. Twenny – two hour. He no ding-ding, he only look.'

'I'm warnin' you, it's nearly eleven, it's closin'-time. If you don't shove off I'm callin' the police. Insultin' behaviour.' She didn't like to scare them but if she had no customer within ten minutes she might be standing and walking for the next couple of hours. That or back to the telephone which might or might not ring. 'Po-lice. Unnerstan'?'

Already they were moving their shared chair back and bowing. The one who spoke a sort of English was offering a white card.

'Thank you, ladyship. You make consideration. We of your service.'

They were sucked backwards into the scrum. The card said, Imo Tenku Joma, Isotypes & Radiotherm Inc. Spring Bedding. Kudan – Kita 1-chome, Chiyoda-ku, Tokyo. Tel. 03-263-9011. From behind the bar a voice bawled, 'Last orders! Last orders, please!' Mandy felt the pressure against her side increase. She inclined her head away from the gust of Guinness.

'There's a word for your sort,' the septuagenarian said.

Mandy ignored him. A golden god in a T-shirt had caught her eye, and she his. He was lodged in the throng but his glass was raised to her. She lifted her shandy. A Swede? Dane?

'Collaborators. That's what we called 'em. Shaved their 'eads, we did.'

'D'you mind?' She pushed away his hand, the iron fingertips of which were jabbing her leg in emphasis.

'Collaborators.' Jab jab went the returned fingertips. 'Shaved their 'eads in France, that's what we did. Nineteen forty-four. I was there.'

'Pity you didn't stay there.' Mandy swatted the gnarled hand. 'Wou'ja pack it in?'

'Them two was Japs. I can tell. I'd 've 'ad a crack at the Japs but I was wounded. 'Ere.' He had begun unbuttoning his shirt. 'Look.'

'Gawd, thanks all the same,' Mandy said, looking away and into the eyes not of her Viking but of a middle-aged policeman.

He was descending with a pint of beer on to the vacated chair. 'Evening, Mandy.'

'Evenin', Mr Peckover.'

'I'd buy you a drink only if I got up I might not see you again. Until tomorrow.'

'What've I done?'

'I dunno. What've you done?'

'Didn't fink you'd lowered yourself to the pussy patrol.'

'Relax, shweetheart.' This was the inspector's third pint and he was feeling amiable. He had drawn a blank at the Greyhound and the Duke of Edinburgh but here was Mandy. 'Know where I might find Dawn de Nuit?'

'Who?'

'Dawn de Nuit.'

'Never 'eard of 'er.'

'Ann Evans?'

'Who's she?'

'Read the newspapers?'

'Only me 'oroscope.'

'What do the twinkling stars foretell, Mandy?'

'I'm losin' a customer, that's what.'

Peckover shifted in his chair and turned his head. He faced Mandy again. 'Big bloke in the sweat shirt?'

''S'right.'

''E's cadging drinks. You'll 'ave to pay 'im.'

'Might've guessed it. All right then, I'll push off.'

'In a minute. Any Arabs lately?'

'Yur, why not? Free country.'

'Anyone called Zadiq? Mohammed Zadiq?'

'How'd I know? I don't write their names down.'

'They phone you?'

'Or the agency.'

'What're you doing in 'ere? Freelancing?'

''S'right. Makes a change.'

'Could be missing some business.'

'Not likely to pick up much now you're 'ere, am I?'

'Any Arab ever called you to the Regent Tower?'

'You're jokin', I'd never get past the 'all porter.' She bit at skin round a rose-red fingernail. 'Actually I would if it was Arabs. They've got suites. You just say Mr Ali Baba's suite or whoever and you're in. They probably own the 'otel anyway, or they've given the porter an oil well.'

'What do they give you, Mandy?'

'I do all right.'

''Ow did you do,' Peckover said, showing a photograph, 'with this one?'

'Cor.' She regarded the brown eyes and toothpaste smile. 'That 'im then, whoever you said?'

'Know 'im?'

'Wish I did.'

'He's an Arab,' the septuagenarian said, leaning and jabbing a finger in Zadiq's incisors. He grasped Peckover's wrist. 'I can tell 'em all. Arabs, Japs, Yanks. Glad my time's nearly over, that's what I say. This country's finished.'

'This country's all right, grandad,' Peckover said, retrieving his wrist.

He edged and shouldered from the bar and walked along Wardour Street past windows aflame with the gore and passion of cinema posters. In Old Compton Street he paused outside a late-night delicatessen. Something for Miriam? He observed ribbons and whirls of pasta, mysterious sausages, tins of Oriental insects in juice, and cheeses both fluid and granite. He entered, browsed and came out with a tin of chestnut purée which she would not thank him for but which she would eat with her finger, scooping it from the tin in holy silence in front of the telly.

In Frith Street a whisper said, 'Why, Mr Peckover. 'Ello.'

''Ello, Sydney. Touch of flu?'

'Laryngitis and 'ay fever. 'Ad bronchitis last week. I oughta be in bed.'

'You ought to give up smoking.'

Cigarette between his lips, hands in pockets, Sydney trotted alongside. He was five feet three.

'There's word about a certain party and a Barclays Bank, Mr Peckover. I might know a name. Worth a tenner?'

'Phone the Yard, Sydney.'

'C'mon, Mr Peckover. A fiver then. I've got doctors' bills.'

'Go to 'Arley Street, do you?'

'Don't go to the soddin' national 'ealth. Pakkies takin' your temperature, maulin' yer, it ain't proper.'

'Night, Sydney.'

Sydney, mumbling, dropped back among the street lamps. Through the window of a coffee bar Peckover saw

Sleazy Suzy sitting with a bushy youth, God help him. Reflected in the window a grey Jaguar passed. Peckover turned his head but a Jensen following too closely hid the registration. He watched both cars turn into Greek Street.

Couldn't possibly be more than a thousand or so grey Jags in London, Peckover estimated.

'Evenin', Suzy. Mind if I sit down?'

'We was just leavin', Inspector.'

'Inspector?' murmured the bushy youth. 'Yeah, well, see yer.' He dropped a 50p coin on the table and retreated into the street.

'Thanks a million,' said Suzy.

'Any time,' Peckover said cheerily, and showed the photograph.

'No,' said Suzy.

Peckover returned the photograph to his wallet. ''Ow're the Arabs, Suzy?'

'They like 'em fat, fifteen and blonde.' Suzy was skinny, forty and currently blue-rinsed. The last time Peckover had seen her she had been an ochreous desert shade as though hopeful of winning Arabs smitten by nostalgia. 'Not that they ain't thick. Tell 'em you're fifteen they'll sweep you off.'

'Ever been swept off by one called Zadiq?'

'Not if 'e's the one in the photo, more's the pity.'

'One of your colleagues, Dawn de Nuit – know 'er?'

'What sorta name's that?'

'Parisian. Ooh la la.'

'Don't know no Parisians.'

'Ann Evans? Welsh.'

Suzy considered, shook her head. 'That the one got dead in Paddington – the television set?'

'Anyone talking about it?'

'Not to me.'

'But if they do you'll let me know.'

'If I let you know, you'll stop bustin' about frightenin' the customers?'

'Cross my 'eart. So who's fat, fifteen, blonde and popular with Arabs?'

'Dunno. Vanessa knows one or two, or says she does. Don't tell 'er I said so.'

'She at the club?'

'She was in 'ere 'alf hour ago with that blackie, Jeannie. Said she was 'ungry. She likes curry.'

'Star of Delhi?'

'Punjab's closer.'

From outside the Punjab looked shut, as in Peckover's experience Indian and Pakistani restaurants always did. Inside a smell of spices, grease and an Indian in a white jacket greeted him. Through the gloom, beyond a rowdy table of junior clerks and secretaries, he spotted Vanessa and a coloured girl spooning mounds of compost into their mouths. By the partition to the kitchen an unshaven man in a grey suit was pushing a diminutive waiter on the chest and mouthing unintelligibly. Peckover had neither the time nor interest.

'Evenin', Vanessa.' He propped Zadiq against a dish of mango chutney. ''Ave a squint at 'im. Back in a minute.'

He aimed for a tacky curtain. Truculent customer and tiny waiter were now mutually pushing but it was going to be all right; from behind the partition had arrived a very large Indian, a cousin of the tiny Indian. Peckover held to the walls as he negotiated the vertical steps into darkness and damp. He groped along a tunnel, past un-inviting doors and side-tunnels and into the ill-lit gent's (Arsenal Poofters OK, read the solitary graffito). He relieved himself, rinsed his hands under the single cold tap and groped back. By the partition the large and small Indians were pushing the unshaven man who was pushing back and saying, 'Bloody sauce.' A complaint about the cooking? Peckover wondered.

'Bloody sauce. I've got rights. Where's your passport?'

The coloured girl was a beauty, black as coal and clad in an even blacker gymnast's outfit. Vanessa had put on weight. She was considerably older than fifteen and her hair was piled in a nimbus thundercloud supported by clamps and rivets but she might fairly have been called fat.

'Feelin' better, Mr Peckover?'

'Don't be cheeky,' Peckover said. 'Introduce us.'

'Jeannie – Inspector Peckover. Inspector Peckover – Jeannie.'

Jeannie, expressionless, spooned compost into her mouth.

'Know 'im?' Peckover said, taking the photo.

'Can't say as we do,' said Vanessa.

Peckover looked at Jeannie for confirmation. The girls sat with their backs to the wall beneath a dusty print of snow-capped peaks. Jeannie was shovelling onto her plate yellow rice spiked with scraps of silver paper, stick-insects and hard greenish droppings; then lumpy compost atop the rice. He had to say, 'Jeannie?' She shook her magnificent black head and began to stir with a rotary motion.

There sounded behind Peckover a bump, a grunt and rattling crockery. One of the secretaries from the rowdy table gave a little cry of alarm. Heads which were not too British and embarrassed to turn turned. From one table a commanding Raj accent called, 'That's quite enough, can we have an end to it!'

'Bloody liberty,' the unshaven man was panting, now on the floor with the tiny waiter sprawled on his chest. The big cousin was trying to pull the unshaved man's shoes off. 'Show us your passports!'

'God's sake,' said Peckover, standing up.

He pushed the waiters aside, dragged the unshaved man to his feet and frog-marched him from the restaurant. On the pavement he gave a parting tweak to the man's arm. 'Come back in 'ere tonight,' Peckover said, 'and I'll unscrew your 'ead – right?'

'Ow!'

'Got it?'

'Got it – ow!'

Ignoring the eyes of the diners, Peckover returned to his seat. His breathing was a little quick.

'Who needs Steve McQueen?' Vanessa asked him, and she giggled. 'Tell you what, Mr Peckover. You should've been a policeman.'

The unsmiling waiter stood above him offering a menu. The tiny one was gathering cutlery from the floor. No one offered thanks.

'Pint of beer – lager if it's all you've got.' What, he wondered, about laws on drinking without eating? Would the waiter be informed? 'And a couple of poppadums.'

'Watching your weight, Mr Peckover?'

'You're cheeky, Vanessa, you'll be cheeky with the wrong bloke one day.'

Neither girl knew Dawn de Nuit. Or Ann Evans. They knew some Arabs but not by name or the one in the photo or the name Zadiq. Simpler to go round the agencies, which Long would have done already, Peckover thought. Someone had to know Zadiq. Dawn de Nuit, six months in the big city, would hardly have been the only one.

Drinking lager, nibbling poppadums, he listened to Vanessa telling a story about a South African client who had wanted to marry her and take her back to South Africa. She began a second story about a German who had pressed religious tracts on her but Jeannie interrupted. Peckover had believed Jeannie was dead. She had not once spoken and having polished her plate with a chapati she had sat back, motionless, beautiful in death, the sepia pools which were her eyes dazed and unseeing.

'Fu'in' foreigners, can't move y'arse for'm, fu'in' all

over, ain' they?' The sepia eyes glinted, the incomparable breasts shivered with passion beneath the gymnast's outfit. Peckover had not heard such cockney since a series of Sunday radio readings in which an actor talented in Bermondsey patois had brought the Bible to the people. The black stretch fabric of the gymnast's gear strained and creaked. 'Ship'm all aht, ship'm 'ome, blee'in' rubbish, 'swot they are, ship'm aht an' pull the fu'in' plug!'

As abruptly as she had come alive Jeannie relapsed into death. Sole evidence of the outburst were the dwindling spasms of her torso and a whiff of mutton vindaloo. Vanessa giggled.

'Jeannie likes politics,' she said.

'National Front?'

'You can say that again.' She giggled louder. 'Got 'er bra on too. You should see 'er without.'

'Who'd be top of the pops with the Arabs, Vanessa?'

'Rifty has her share. They flew her out to Kuwait or somewhere. But she's got her own agency now.'

True, thought Peckover. Rifty. He swallowed the last of the lager. 'Brewer Street?' he said.

'Wouldn't know, Mr Peckover.'

'Don't rouse your friend, it's post-curry coma. Best let it take its course.'

Peckover placed a silver contribution on the table and left the Punjab to no applause. He made a right turn in the direction of Brewer Street. Twelve-thirty. Desultory figures lounged in the doorways of the strip clubs. The temperature could not have dropped much below eighty. A plain police car holding three heavies dawdled past.

Rifty liked girls but for a living she had taken on all comers. Judging by her trinkets and Mayfair pad she had taken on not a few of the oil princes and sons of oil princes who swanned in with sand in their moccasins. She might well have a thought about Zadiq. She might even have known Ann Evans. She had given shelter and comfort to many girls who had arrived in London with a suitcase, ten pounds and nowhere to go.

Hopeful about Rifty, Peckover cut through St Anne's Court. There was little light and nobody about, apart from the treading feet behind him. He turned far too slowly. He heard as well as cried out at the rush of air. But he felt hardly anything. What little light there was, someone had simply turned it out.

CHAPTER V

Dreams of blood-coloured shapes and dark seas swam, faded and swam again into focus. The next rational thought of Detective-Inspector Peckover was: Have I lost my memory?

He believed he was in a prone position but he was not greatly interested and he did not feel up to opening his eyes. There were voices. He was moderately comfortable apart from his head.

Dense drunk imbecile policeman. He'd been in a fracas or two in the course of his career. Most coppers had. In vice anyway. Tapped on the head too, though always up to now in what was laughingly called a fair fight. Twice tapped unconscious, briefly. Eerie sort of experience. Never lost his memory though. Not so far.

But it could happen. Happened to old Jackie Jones when the Petty brothers jumped him. Jackie Jones couldn't remember his name.

Amnesia.

Freesia. Seizure. Polynesia.

Henry Peckover. Henry Charles Peckover.

He remembered St Anne's Court long ago. Going to see Rifty, was it? Some derelict he'd thrown out of somewhere.

Cheeky Vanessa. A black dish with boobs. Jeannie.
His head throbbed abominably.

So much for medical science. Likely some student
experimenting with his first bandage. How long had he
been here in bed? Poor Miriam.

Peckover sniffed for the hospital smell of boiled cabbage,
anaesthetics.

'Henry?'

He opened his eyes and looked up into the raw face of
Ken Long.

He had hoped he might have been among friends.
Shifting his gaze he recognized a blue uniform but not the
face. A second blue uniform. He was not in a hospital bed
either. More a settee. No white coats. All policemen.
Sergeant Faulds in his silk striped shirt.

Bloody Vine Street. Back room of the Vine Street cop
shop. He'd sunk a beer or two here in his time.

He levered himself up on to his elbows and lifted his
wrist to his eyes. Ten minutes to one.

'Easy, Henry,' someone said.

'Did you see him?' Long said.

'One or more than one?' said Faulds.

'Ambulance here!' someone called.

'Tell 'em to wait!' called back Long in a voice which reopened Peckover's skull. Soft as a houri's touch, Long said,
'Quick description, Henry. We'll have him.'

'Or them,' Faulds said.

'Didn't see 'im,' Peckover said, and winced.

'You saw something, a glimpse,' said Long.

'Leave him, he's out, he didn't see,' said someone.

'Stinkin', get a whiff,' a background voice said. 'Percy
Bysshe, stoned to the eyeballs.'

'Probably fell out of a window.'

'I shot a copper in the air, he fell to earth near Leicester
Square.'

'Sssh!'

'What was he wearing?' Long said.

'St Anne's Court,' Peckover said. 'There was a geezer in the Punjab.'

'Where?'

'From the start, Henry,' Faulds said. 'Think back. Who've you been upsetting?'

'How about Phil Mackie, Henry?'

'The Robertsons?'

'Big, medium?'

'Wouldn't be anyone to do with Greenmead and Zadiq and that lot, would it, Henry?'

'You've upset someone, old son. Think.'

'He didn't nick anything, Henry. You've got your wallet. It's some bloke knew you.'

'Punjab,' Peckover said. 'Threw this geezer out. Disturbance. Medium, grey suit, scruffy white shirt, no tie, needed a shave, thin mouth, watery eyes, posh accent, seen better times. Didn't seem the type.'

He closed his eyes and heard rustling, footsteps, doors banging, voices: 'Thin mouth, watery eyes, grey suit . . .' Where, he wanted to know, was sodding Terry Sutton, supposed to be his right hand, only seen him twice in six weeks, jigging off after bank cards, so he said. Probably got a girl.

'Did you get his name, Henry?'

'Nothing. Wouldn't 'ave thought 'im the type. Can't tell, though. Unshaved.'

'Could've shaved by now.'

'Grown a beard by the time you lot get after 'im,' Peckover said. Dark seas and shapes were closing in. 'I don't feel so good. Listen, tell Sutton, Terry Sutton, if he exists, tell 'im to get on to the DC. The missing bit of Molehill. Got to be an enquiry.'

'What enquiry?'

'Easy, Henry. You're going to be lifted. You'll be all right.'

'Henry, where did you say? Where you threw this bloke out of?'

'Punjab.'

'We go to the Punjab?'

'God's sake, not the Punjab Punjab. You don't need visas. The Punjab in Greek Street.'

He was being lifted, carried, then lowered on to his side. He tried to turn on to his back but hands prevented him. 'Hold it there, mate. Won't be long.' A hand held his head. He was airborne.

'Tell Miriam not,' he started to say, then went to sleep.

In the ambulance he opened his eyes. He recalled a grey Jaguar.

'There was a grey Jag,' he said.

'Yes?'

'Nothing,' he said.

When he was on his feet he was going to be pretty cross, he believed. Juvenile but he'd not say no to a minute or two with his cosher on his own. Just himself and the cosher where he could see him.

If the lads got nowhere with the Punjab geezer he might try the grey Jag himself.

Except that he could not remember the registration of the Jag anyway.

Not until two days later did word of the coshing of a fraud squad detective reach Alderman Beeston.

The news arrived casually. Had Beeston not been a gregarious animal – mayor-elect, chairman of the police committee, past president of the Rotary Club, full-time estate agent, with acquaintances in a variety of walks of life and friends in such areas as Whitehall, including the Home Office – he might not have heard for three days or longer.

'Thanks,' he said into the telephone and hung up.

If the inspector had been coshed hard enough for him to

be retired or shunted to welfare or organizing the police
ball or wherever high-risk policemen might be shunted
for their safety's sake – fine. If not, if he recovered, he still
might not recover his nerve. But he might. The hue and
cry was going to be hot enough without one coshed and
vengeful rozzer leading the charge.

Beeston's depression was deep. Zadiq had telephoned
accusing him of blackmail, of threatening to expose
Zadiq and Greenmead with documentary evidence sent
to the director of public prosecutions and to the press if
he did not pay up. Pay up how much and how long the
blackmail had been going on, Zadiq had refused to say.
He had refused to say even where he was telephoning
from, though at three in the morning it might have been
anywhere from here to Pretoria. Secretive bloody smiling
pipsqueak wog. Smiling all the fifty thousand miles along
the telephone line. In Beeston's experience the more
Zadiq smiled the more dangerous he was.

Worse if anything, on the evening of his return from
Rimini an Inspector Long had turned up with another
copper and an engraved watch. He'd been able to satisfy
them he'd never set eyes on the watch in his life, that his
initials were not BB anyway, they were FBB, F for Frank,
Frank by name and Frank by nature, and on the evening
they were so fascinated about he'd been at the golf dance
until two-thirty and plenty of witnesses to that. He must
have satisfied them. They'd not been back.

Still.

He telephoned Willie McLeod but was granted only
the croak.

'Not 'ere, is 'e? 'Asn't been 'ere for two days. Try the
dogs. White City tonight, innit?'

He telephoned Thomas Mountain. Thirty minutes
later he was picking his way through rubble, over planks
and around craters like dried-up waterholes in the out-
back. The day was as hot as any that summer. The cranes

lifted and lowered, the labourers were gravy-coloured. Thomas and Rupert Mountain were waiting in the foreman's hut. The foreman was absent.

'Maniacs,' Beeston said, breathing hard. 'You mad? What're you trying to prove?'

Thomas Mountain scowled. 'Nice, very nice. That's charming, that is. If you know something we don't p'raps you'll let us in on it.'

'You know. That Yard man who's been coshed. Peckover. The new one in fraud. You put Willie McLeod up to it.'

'Crap,' Rupert Mountain said.

'Shut up,' said the father. He was seated in shirt-sleeves on the only chair. A zig-zag of sweat, moving southward from the bald dome and down the forehead, had paused at a wrinkle. 'When did we put who up to what?'

'Don't give me that. Couple of days ago he was done. He might've been killed.'

'Really? Had any visits?'

'Not yet.'

'No questions?'

'No.' Long, the red-faced inspector with the watch, he was something else and no one knew or needed to know about Long. Less everyone knew about everything the better. 'What about yourself?'

'What about me?'

'Questions?'

'I don't expect any,' Mountain said. 'Because I never put anyone up to anything. All right?'

Beeston glowered. His eyes moved to Rupert.

'First I heard of it so don't look at me,' Rupert said.

'Leaves you,' Thomas Mountain said. 'So what is it, your aldermanship, you're trying to prove?'

'What's that supposed to mean?'

'Just that if anyone slipped Willie a bundle to do the

footpad bit on a copper, you did. Like you paid him to rough up that reporter, the Australian, Carter.'

'That, for your information, is slander. You've no evidence.'

'Who's asking for evidence? I'm talking facts. You had Carter done. Now it's this Peckover. And while we're talking straight for a change, I suppose you've not been suggesting to Zadiq I'm trying to blackmail him?'

'Look, Mountain, I've had enough. Who said Zadiq was being blackmailed?'

'He did. And you know it. Because when he rang me he said he'd already rung you and you were saying you knew nothing. Now I think about it, Beeston, wouldn't surprise me if you'd hinted to him I might be the one putting the screws on.'

'Out of your mind.'

'You're a devious bugger. What're you up to?'

'Shut your face.' Beeston's own face had begun to show signs of high blood-pressure. 'Peckover started snooping and you paid Willie McLeod to warn him off. Like you pay everyone. You're round the twist.'

'You'd better buzz off. I'm not listening to this.'

'You never do listen. Just barge ahead scattering any-one who gets in your way.'

'Some of us have to barge. Others just sit on their arses and collect. But I never barged a busy and neither did Rupert or he'd be out on his ear and he knows it. So unless you've something more interesting to talk about, Mr Alderman, you can clear out.'

'I'll clear out when I'm ready.'

'Suit y'self. C'mon, Rupert. Funny smell in here.' Thomas Mountain stood and picked up his white helmet. 'There's some of us has to make a living.'

'You fed Willie McLeod a bundle to cosh that inspector and you know it!' Beeston said.

'And I'd say you did it but I don't know for sure, and

what damn politics you're playing now, Beeston, Christ knows!' Mountain wiped a hairy forearm over his bald head. 'Course, we could phone McLeod.'

'I have. He's not in.'

Beeston and Mountain glared at each other. Pink suffused the suntan.

Rupert Mountain said, 'Maybe it's nobody. I mean, Soho, night-time, it can happen, it could be anyone.'

'Like who?'

'Like anyone. Louts, druggies. I'm telling you, read the papers, it happens.'

'It happened to a fraud squad copper who happens to have taken over on Greenmead,' Beeston said. 'Ask your father – he knows.'

'I'm taking no more of this,' Thomas Mountain said.

'And who said it was Soho and night-time?' Beeston closed on Rupert Mountain. 'Come on – who?'

'What?'

'Thought you didn't know anything about it!' Beeston's voice was high, far removed from the round tones of the council chamber.

'It was in the paper.'

'What paper? Come on then – what paper?' Beeston took hold of the lapels of Rupert's jacket. 'I said what paper?'

'All right, it wasn't the paper! It was Charlie, he got it from the desk sergeant at Vine Street. They're mates – '

'Charlie? Champagne Charlie is my name! Who's Charlie?'

Beeston released the lapels, placed the flat of his hands on Rupert's chest and pushed.

'Leave him alone!' Thomas Mountain said, and he pushed Beeston.

Beeston fell against the wall of the hut. He lumbered back and pushed Thomas Mountain, sending him sideways into the table. Drawings and pencils skidded across

the floor. The builder swung his white helmet, striking
Beeston with it on the shoulder. Beeston staggered then
came forward again. Builder and alderman fell against
each other like asthmatic bulls, grunting and pushing.

'Stop it!' Rupert cried. He gripped a shoulder of each
combatant.

'I'll settle you!'

'Like you settled that copper!'

'Liar! Take – agh!'

'Aaagh! Would you!'

'Both of you – stop it!'

'Fiver on the baldy,' said Peckover from the doorway.
The wrestling froze into a tableau which after a moment, after held breaths and exhalations, came apart.

'Who the hell are you?' Thomas Mountain panted.

'Peckover. Police. Who the 'ell are you?'

'None o' your damn business. You're trespassing.'

'More 'n likely. You must be Mountain. You're Beeston.
You'll be either Rupert Mountain or the site pimp. A
nastier trio one couldn't wish to meet. Two geriatric con
men and a pampered brat.'

'Here, I don't care who you are, you're not – '

'Shut your mouth or I'll knock your head off.'

The policeman smiled and raised his hat, revealing his
own swathed head. There were no visible pins or knots.
The snowy bandage rode horizontally above the eyebrows, enveloped the crown of the head, dipped over the
ears and curved round the nape of the neck. Peckover
looked like an unfinished Egyptian mummy.

He felt like an Egyptian slave-master about to do someone a damage. He had been visited in Islington by too
many colleagues. Two more suspects had been questioned
and two-thirds of them already released. The unshaved
man had been Eric Vere Wall, former stalwart in the
defunct League of Empire Loyalists, now drawing un-
employment benefit and on the night of the Punjab un-

deniably locked in his hostel from 11.50 p.m. until morning. The deputy commander, after a token word of sympathy, had reprimanded him for discharging himself from hospital against express medical advice. Yesterday evening, attempting to dress, he had fallen over and numbed his coccyx, though it seemed to be all right today. Miriam had said she would leave him if he tried to get up again. He had warned that he would leave her if she did not stop fussing and clear off to her archaeologists. As soon as the door had closed behind her and he had risen, shaved and dressed, the telephone had rung.

At least it had been Terry Sutton. He had heard himself shouting into the telephone that he didn't care if he was in Pago-Pago, he didn't care if five million American Express cards were forged and circulating, if he didn't get back and have the registration HLM 559N traced by nine o'clock he personally would bind him to the railway and dance a hornpipe while the American Express rolled over him at one hundred mph.

If he had left his bed for anywhere it ought to have been the fraud office at the Yard. Enough work there. The typed report on the coshing. The forms for the enquiry into Molehill's missing part five. Routine calls on Molehill. Rifty the tart. A visit to the sacked planning officer, York or whoever he was. Another to the night porter at the Regent Tower. Ames-Clegg, though he could wait. Zadiq. In which world capital was Zadiq flashing his qualifications now? London maybe?

None of this had awakened interest in Peckover.

He looked at his watch as a change from looking at the alderman and two Mountains. Sutton would not have anything for him by noon. He might by mid-afternoon.

'Don't let me stop you,' he said. 'Thieves falling out?'

'You've no right – ' Rupert Mountain began.

'Shut up,' said Thomas Mountain. 'Told you, Peckover, whatever your name is, you're trespassing. I'll see your search warrant.'

'You'll see moons and stars. See what it's like on the receiving end. Was it you?'

'Was it me what?'

'A hammer? One of your navvy's shovels?'

'You watch it, Peckover. I don't know what you're on about but just watch it.'

'No, unlikely, you're past it. All that emotion, you'd 'ave 'ad an 'eart attack. What about you?'

Rupert Mountain, startled, looked ready to spring to attention.

'Yes, you, Sylvia. You with the eyelashes. Bumped anyone with a rock recently?'

'You've no right!' Rupert Mountain said. 'I'm not – '

'No, you wouldn't either. Rights, rights. Some sort of lawyer, are you? Democratic League of Defence Against Coppers' Questions? Who's got rights? Polish your fingernails, Sylvia.' Peckover eyed Beeston. 'Leaves you.'

The alderman was smoothing his hair, straightening his golf club tie.

Peckover said, 'It's a fair old jump from your council chamber to dark nights in Soho.'

'I've no quarrel with you, Inspector.' Beeston was mild as milk. 'You mentioned lawyers. I believe, you in your present mood – '

'Oh yes? What mood's that?'

' – mine might recommend me to say nothing.'

'I believe 'e probably would. Where is 'e – prison?'

'I'd not stand for that,' Thomas Mountain said. 'Who does he – ?'

'It's all right, Tom.' Placatory, calming the council chamber, the alderman held his palms shoulder-high. 'I'm willing to forget these innuendoes and I think the inspector knows it. Exactly what you're trying to say, Mr Peckover, I've not the least idea. Judging from the bandages and insinuations you've perhaps been hit?

You're naturally resentful, not on peak form.'

'I'm on very peak form. As you surmise, sir, I 'ave per-haps been 'it. But my God, I'm on very peak form indeed.'

'I – '

'Peak form enough to recognize a stinker, Beeston. A talker and a stinker. A creepy-crawly.'

'There's no point continuing with this,' Beeston said.

He looked round the hut as if for a hat or briefcase. Peckover returned his own hat to his white head and stepped forward.

'I'm the one decides whether there's any point,' he breathed in Beeston's face. 'You'll be 'appy to know you and I are going to be seeing each other fairly regularly from now on. So be in. What car d'you drive?'

'Mercedes. What business – '

'Registration?'

'PBY Six-six-one J.'

'What else?'

'Marina. AHJ Four-two-seven B.'

'You?' Peckover said, side-stepping in front of Rupert Mountain.

'Rover – the company car. And a Volkswagen. I don't see – '

'Registration?'

'I've had enough of this nonsense,' Thomas Mountain said, picking up his helmet.

'Quiet, you silly man.' Peckover side-stepped again. 'And don't think you're going anywhere. 'Ow many company cars then?'

'I don't have to take this,' said Mountain.

'I might remind you, Mr Peckover,' Beeston said, 'we've read a fair amount in the press recently about behaviour by certain police officers. There are two enquiries going on right now into planted evidence. As chairman of East Middlesex police committee I'm not unfamiliar – '

'Ha!' Peckover in two strides was back in front of Beeston. 'Warning me off, are you, Mr Chairman?' He took hold of both the alderman's ears and twisted. 'Certain behaviour? What sort of certain behaviour would that be?'

Beeston's hold on the inspector's wrists achieved nothing. The ears twisted, the alderman's knees bent. Mouth open, eyes screwed shut, he succeeded in not crying out.

'You can't do that, we're all witnesses!' Thomas Mountain shouted.

'All complaints in writing, sir,' Peckover said, twisting. 'Put it in writing and send it in.'

Alderman Beeston was on his knees, his face contorted. Peckover let go and walked from the hut.

CHAPTER VI

'Gonna wash that ham right outa the air, gonna wash that –'

'You've had too much,' said the girl, and tittered. 'Where are the lights?'

'Economy drive. Landlord's contribution to the balance of, balance of –'

'Go on, keep going. Which floor are you?'

'Balance of power.'

She steered him by the elbow. On the first-floor landing he found an untousled area of forehead which he kissed.

'Gonna wash that ham right out the air,' they sang in unison.

Never was a bouncy song more lugubriously sung. On the second-floor landing he slid the window open, protruded a shaggy head and asked the sparse traffic in the Earl's Court Road below, 'Have you no beds to go to?'

The enquiry gave her a momentary pause, a regret and a frisson. Never mind, he was fun and big, she'd met him a dozen or more times on jobs and the Pill conquered all. He wasn't as tipsy as he was pretending to be either. As long as there was toothpaste. And she had worked well on the train crash at Deptford. She deserved something even if it were only a chocolate and someone to hold her hand.

On the third floor he fumbled with a key. The battered suede jacket across his shoulder started to slide and its adjustment took time. He found another spare area of forehead to kiss, opened the door and switched on the light.

'Turn that light out, I've got a headache,' said a man with a bandaged head from the armchair beside the television.

'Who d'you think you are?'

'The light!'

Ross Carter switched off the light. The table lamp on the far side of the room shed a roseate glow over bachelor disorder: unwashed mugs and plates on the table, newspapers and mugs on the floor, on the sofa crumbs, sliced bread and jammy knives. The television screen was extinguished. The man in the armchair had a can of beer in his hand and the *Evening Standard* on his lap.

'Name's Peckover. Police. Who's that with you?'

'Just going,' said the girl. 'Night, Ross. Thanks.'

'Hold on, he's not staying.' Ross Carter ushered the girl into the flat and closed the door. 'How the hell did you get in?'

'Abracadabra. You should change your lock. There's a free advisory service, enquire at your nearest police station.'

'Bloody liberty. Would you have anything like a scroll or a photograph? Been a while since anyone broke in here and said they were police.'

Peckover delved and brought out his warrant card.

'You're Carter?'

'Right, mate. And this is my flat.'

'Your name, miss?'

'Isobel Wood. I'm just leaving.'

'The fuzz is leaving, he's got a headache.' Carter put an arm round the girl. 'You're making coffee because the good word in these parts is no one makes coffee like you, if there is any. What a story! "Scotland Yard Man Breaks Into Reporter's Pad After Brain Operation!" '

'No story, Carter,' the policeman said.

'Wanna bet? Two against one.'

Carter handed back the warrant card and tossed his jacket on to the arm of the sofa. He guided Dizzy Wood through a minefield of mugs and magazines and into a hopeless kitchen. Peckover heard the pair talking. He had assumed Carter would return to the flat alone. Why had he assumed that? He had assumed Carter would have been back before two in the morning. On what basis?

'Who's she work for?'

'*The Times*,' Carter said. Hands on hips he stood above the policeman in a not entirely unmenacing attitude. 'What a story!'

'No story, sport. Or one night you'll come back 'ere and strike a match and blow yourself up. Left leg in the river, right leg in Camden Town, arse in Melbourne. Or wherever you're from. 'Ave a beer.'

'You're a bloody weird copper. Force your way into a private –'

'You invited me in. Stoned you were. And the girl.'

' – and now it's the tragic accident to shut the bugger up. You're the one writes poetry, right?'

'Not any more. Taken the pledge. 'Ere, Foster's lager, don't tell me it's the wrong stuff, I went out specially.' The policeman fished by the side of the armchair and brought up a partially demolished twelve-pack. ''Ave a cold tube, cobber.'

'Don't mind. Don't mind if you get to the point then clear out either. You're a weird one.' Carter took a can and sat on the sofa among crockery and knives; an amiable, unkempt six-and-a-half feet of alternating energy and sloth in jeans, gingham shirt and a belt with a buckle in the shape of a steer's head. 'No offence but I've already got a guest. Couldn't you have phoned first?'

'Who's talking? The police and the press never phone. They arrive.' He turned a page of the *Evening Standard*. 'Fleet Street must be quite a step up.'

'Fleet Street's soft after that lot up at Greenmead – if that's what you're after. No council stuff here. It's in the contract. Ross Carter, Strictly No Council Stuff.' He popped the beer can. 'Once bitten.'

'Or once thumped.'

'Too true, mate. Looks like you should know.' Carter slid into a horizontal posture, shoulders and back flat on the sofa, bottom unsupported in space, legs spread-eagled. 'Turn down a backhander?'

'Beg your pardon?'

'Come on – couple of hundred? Two-fifty? A century I was offered but the rate's probably higher for a copper.' He tipped the can and swallowed. 'Can't see why it should be.'

'No,' Peckover agreed.

'You've been landed with Greenmead, they've clobbered you and you want me to testify. How'm I doing?'

'Close. Some of it.'

'What about a deal? You give me the story about your head, exclusive, and I'll think about turning up for any trial.' A coffee aroma floated in from the kitchen 'How many stitches?'

'Who offered you the 'undred?'

'Mountain. Any sense I'd have taken it, would have saved me a hiding. Probably it finished up with the editor anyway. A first instalment for forgetting the deep pockets on our East Middlesex Council and elsewhere.'

'Where elsewhere?'

'Don't be coy. I was in the front line, remember?"
Carter put a hand on his belly and released an anti-
podean belch. 'Some coppers take what's going.'

'Which coppers take what's going, Carter?'

'Where's my story of copper-bashing? How many
stitches?'

'Sixteen. Which coppers?'

'Wouldn't say no to another cold one.'

Peckover steered the dwindling twelve-pack across the
carpet with his foot. Carter popped a can.

'I'm guessing, I'm your ignorant foot-in-the-door man,
but it has to go fairly high. Why didn't your deputy
commander get those first transcripts to the director of
public prosecutions until March? All my early interviews
with Beeston before he clammed up? Why'd the public
prosecutor's office wait half a year before coming down
from Olympus and saying there was no case? Why didn't
your Mr Farnsworth get his finger out? I'd say he pocketed
his share. Ditto the East Middlesex chief constable and
his gang. Beeston and Mountain were shelling out every
month.'

'Not Zadiq?'

'Course Zadiq. Zadiq's where it all starts. Was it his
chauffeur clobbered you?'

'Who?'

'Zadiq's chauffeur. An actual Neanderthal Arab.'

'How clean would you guess the MP is – Ames-Clegg?
Your stories in the *Advertiser* didn't say much.'

'Never got near him, only once. I'd say he was clean like
a used nappy's clean.' Carter swallowed from the can. 'So
it wasn't Zadiq's boy or you'd be dead. Willie McLeod?'

'Willie McLeod's the muscle, is 'e?'

'Mean you didn't even see him?' Carter's laugh was like
a snapped banjo string. He tilted his chin and pointed to

a pale line beneath his jaw. He pushed back his hair at the temple, fingered his scalp and said, 'Seven stitches, I don't even compete.' He dragged up a jeans leg and displayed a hairless patch on the shin. 'That was your actual pommy boot.'

'McLeod's not strictly a pom. Must be a Scot.'

'You don't say so. How extraordinarily interesting, old top.'

'You should've come to us. We'd 'ave got 'im on GBH.'

'And the Greenmead pack 'd have paid number two on the muscles list to break my other leg.'

'Why didn't you go after 'im yourself? You're a big lad.'

'Big but soft. One day maybe. With a few mates, like twelve or twenty bricklayers. They'd need to be Irish. Twenty Irish bricklayers should do it. McLeod's a pro.' Carter scowled. One unjeaned shin with a hairless patch gleamed in the bordello glow of the table lamp. 'Anyway, now you can get him for grievous bodily harm yourself, can't you? And assaulting a busybody? Jesus, they hang you for that! Why aren't you out bringing him in?'

'Reasons.' Such as, brooded Peckover, never having heard of Willie McLeod until half a minute ago.

The grey Jag had to have been stolen, Terry Sutton had reported at tea-time. The registration HLM 559N belonged, or had belonged, to a stolen Hillman belonging to a Mr Walter Clacton, a Kidderminster carpet manufacturer who had died in April aged eighty-three. Peckover pinched his earlobe. Had he ever heard of Willie McLeod? Who was the lout, a boxer, boxed somewhere and assaulted a traffic warden?

Willie McLeod sounded Scotch enough. Not a drop is sold till it's seven years old. Could be Bethnal Green, though. Couldn't tell these days. Could be Kirkapakawak, Saskatchewan.

The girl from *The Times* had come in with a tray not

only of coffee but of welsh rabbit, potato crisps and rem-
nants of a box of dates flecked with fur. She looked about
for tray-space, discovered it on the carpet between
Peckover and the reporter and placed the tray thereon.

She said to Carter, 'D'you have a loo?'

'Dizzy, you're beautiful,' Carter said, pointing over his
shoulder to a door beyond the table lamp.

She went through the door with her handbag. Peckover
stood up and said, 'What was the name of Zadiq's
chauffeur?'

'Genghis Khan. What about my story?'

'I'll be in touch. Might 'ave something for you later.'

'Yeah, I bet.'

'Exclusive.' The policeman arranged a brown hat over
the white bandage. 'Keep the Fosters, sport, what there
is. A small backhander from the police to the press.'

He went out. Off-stage a cistern rumbled. Miss Wood
came in smelling of Colgate and Shalimar.

'Why don't you either pull that other leg up or that one
down?' She kneeled and poured coffee. 'It's not the hairy
leg, just that you look off-balance.'

'I feel off-balance.' He pushed the jeans leg down.
'I'm not saying he's bent, he's too weird to be bent. He'd
never have lasted.'

'I wouldn't trust him with a Green Shield Stamp,'
Dizzy said.

Ross Carter, abstracted, took the coffee in one hand
and her hand in his other.

Detective-Inspector Peckover honked, flashed his in-
dicator, overtook the ambulance and accelerated to sixty
along the Commercial Road. Pencilled along the margin
of the *Evening Standard* on the seat beside him was the
address offered by records.

At three o'clock in the morning the road was empty. If
a squad car spotted him he'd race, give 'em their money's

worth, then stop and bawl them out. He'd take names and numbers and blast them. He was in the mood.

He had been locked in the same mood since an occasion in St Anne's Court two nights ago. It was not the pain but the humiliation. The nerve of the bloke. The gall. The humiliation of being slugged so expertly you never even saw him.

Stepney East. Through a red light into Limehouse at sixty-two. It was not the humiliation either. When did being humiliated hurt anyone? It was the sodding ache to the flesh and bone beneath the bandage.

I let them off too easily, the builders and our jovial alderman, Peckover thought. Well, time enough. They could wait.

Why when he'd done nothing and knew nothing get coshed in the first place? What did he know that all the former fraud compilers of the Molehill dunghill hadn't known? And why two nights ago at half twelve? Why not the night before or next week?

Deduction? The Greenmead pack or someone in the Greenmead pack was frightened he did know something. Or might be about to discover something. Or was sailing too close to something in visiting – who? A clutch of Soho tarts?

Farnsworth?

Farnsworth too could wait. He'd come to a conclusion or two about Farnsworth before the reporter lad had tossed the name into the hat.

East India Dock Road. The lights of trucks and juggernauts disgorged from the Blackwall Tunnel blazed towards speeding Peckover. To his right, Poplar and the docks. He had been a boy here. Since the blitz and the burgeoning of post-war tower blocks he could recognize about half of it.

Not a copper to be seen. If he met a riot or a smash-and-grab, fine, let them grab and smash and riot.

He wanted no coppers where he was going. Not that there'd be a hope in hell of Willie-boy being in, not with the Yard scouring London for a copper-basher. His parents' house. According to records he'd had a place in Hoxton but not any more. Clean for two years, since an incident with a traffic warden. No interest in him at the Yard. No address. Not with former fraud man Farnsworth as compiler-in-chief of the Molehill file.

Peckover slowed, swung into Abbot Road and made three false turns before discovering the two-up, two-down brick and dinginess of Ensign Terrace. Only one of the street lamps had not been smashed and that stood at the far end of the street.

The blitz had ignored Ensign Terrace. All social, economic and cultural developments since the industrial revolution, with the exception of television and the internal combustion engine, had ignored Ensign Terrace. The houses sprouted television aerials. With few gaps, cars lined the kerb of both pavements.

There was no gap near the McLeods at No. 26. No grey Jaguars. Peckover had to wind down the window and shine a flashlight to make sure he had the right number. Gloom, unlit windows, a delivery van and a file of cars on the never-never. Double-parked, he switched off the lights and engine and stepped into the street. Ensign Terrace was like a street closed off because of plague. The only sounds were somewhere a baby crying and the muffled juggernauts along the East India Dock Road.

Peckover shone his torch and pressed a bell which gave no ring. The door had an appearance of having been scraped in readiness for paint which no one had got round to applying. There were unwashed milk bottles and low down on the brick the chalked declaration, *cliff luves sumantha.* He knocked hard on the door. The door vibrated, the knocking echoed along Ensign Terrace.

He stepped back and switched off the flashlight, which was police issue, a foot long and clothed in an unyielding rubbery composition. He had no need of the flashlight, the night was not black, but should Willie McLeod be available it might come in handy. Willie-boy had been a prize-fighter until two or three years ago, records had revealed. Peckover stepped forward, knocked again and stepped back. A light went on in one of the two upstairs windows.

The curtain moved, the window creaked up. A face appeared, half-hidden by hair in rat's-tails.

'Wha' is it?' croaked the face.

'Is Willie McLeod in?'

'No 'e ain't! Who the 'ell is it?'

'Where can I find 'im?'

'Who d'yer fink y'are wakin' people up this hour?'

The window slid shut, the curtain fell back into place.

'Hey!' Peckover shouted.

He strode forward and hammered on the door. He moved back off the pavement into the space between the bumpers of two cars and watched the window.

The window opened. Abuse crackled from the crone's streaked face. Peckover waited for the pause for breath, then called up, 'I owe 'im money!'

'Yer wha'?'

'Willie, if 'e's there, I owe 'im money!'

"Ow much?'

'Fifty!'

'Wha's yer name?'

'Beeston!'

'Never 'eard of yer!'

'Tell 'im it's Beeston!'

"Old on!'

The rat's-tails disappeared. The light from the window illuminated a patch of street and within the patch the inspector from fraud. He tugged the brim of the brown

hat lower and stepped on to the pavement. Head cocked,
he listened for sounds from the other side of the door.
His eyes shifted from the door to the lighted window and
back to the door. He adjusted the grip on the flashlight.
Its obese head of glass, chrome and rubber fell, lifted and
fell again, tapping the palm of his hand.

They were heavy sleepers along the rest of Ensign
Terrace. Even the baby had ceased crying.

The tapping of the flashlight quickened. Peckover's eyes
flickered upward, from side to side and straight ahead to
the door. These terraced houses had yards at the rear,
walled or fenced; outside privy, dustbins, rubbish, a cast-
out roll of linoleum, a square of soil for tomatoes, another
for the cat. He backed into the middle of the road and
looked one way, then the other.

No one. A plague-deserted street. Bring out your dead.

The open window remained empty. Peckover came
forward to the house and tried the doorhandle. It was
loose but it held. He stepped to his right, fingered the
frame of the downstairs window, then strained at it. The
window held too.

"E ain't 'ere so piss orf!' croaked the voice from the
upstairs window. The window slid shut.

Peckover slammed the flashlight against his palm. He
hoisted a leg and kicked the door with the sole of his shoe.
'Hey!' he cried to the closed window. He snatched up a
milk bottle, ran into the road and bowled the bottle high,
hard and overarm. To his surprise the aim was true.
The bottle smashed through the lighted window. Peckover ducked, arms across his face, cowering from thoughts
of splintered glass.

Several windows distant a second window lit up and
almost immediately a third. 'What's goin' on?' shouted a
voice, not the crone's. At the crone's smashed window the
rat's-tails appeared, the remains of the window lifted. A
missile which Peckover failed to identify curved in his

direction and struck the road. Shrieked abuse followed. He watched a car start to pull away from the kerb at the far end of the street.

'You wait there, I'll sort you out!' shouted the voice which was not the crone's.

Six or seven windows were now lit up. A door opened across the street and a shaft of light from the hall advanced over the pavement and into the road. Peckover ran through the shaft of light towards the car.

The car might have been a Jaguar and grey but the solitary street lamp illumined not the car but an area beyond it. Motionless now, silent, the car pointed approximately in Peckover's direction but askew, in the road's middle, as though in contemplation. Either it had stalled or was considering reversing. Or the driver was going to run.

The engine started again, the headlights came on. Peckover raced, narrowing the gap from forty yards, to thirty, to twenty. The car accelerated towards him.

Peckover halted. He switched on his flashlight, pointed it and shouted, 'Stop!' The car approached with a crescendo of engine-roar and blinding headlights. Peckover held his ground.

Me or him, he had time to think.

He threw himself sideways. Simultaneously, as though itself lacking the courage, the car braked and swerved in the opposite direction. There sounded a rending of metal. From the ground, hip and leg lodged beneath the wheel of a parked car, Peckover watched a Guy Fawkes night of sparks. The Jaguar was accelerating again. Still accelerating, lighting its way with a single beam, it sped past the double-parked car and cornered on shrilling tyres out of Ensign Terrace.

Peckover collected his hat from the gutter. The flashlight was gone and his hip hurt. With a lop-sided gait he limped in the direction of his car. He lacked confidence

in the atmosphere in Ensign Terrace. Lights shone in the
houses, householders were at windows and in the street.
Feet padded behind him.

"'E's the one!' shrieked a voice. 'There in the 'at!'

'Look at my bleedin' car!' cried another.

A hand grabbed Peckover's jacket collar and almost
tore the jacket from his back. 'Sortin' you out for a start,
tosh!' came a voice in the policeman's ear.

Peckover swung round and punched the face of a man
in slippers and pyjama bottoms. The man fell backwards
in the road.

'There in the 'at!' shrieked the voice from the window.

Peckover climbed into his car and switched on the
engine. At the side of the car a woman in a quilted
dressing-gown was thumping the bonnet and shouting.
Peckover blasted the horn and drove forward fast. He
glimpsed the mangled flank of a Morris Oxford, glass in
the road and a youth with pop eyes and an open mouth.

In the East India Dock Road he cruised at thirty. He
was trembling. When his hand investigated his hip and
leg it discovered a rip which gave access through the
cloth to the leg.

He continued on towards Aldgate, Islington and home.

CHAPTER VII

In spite of the forecast of rain, Detective-Inspector Henry
Peckover decided to spend the day in bed. It was Sunday
and he had awoken sweating from three hours of haunted
dreams in which had recurred a bishop wearing a frock,
blessing him and expressing concern for his spiritual
health.

He could watch the rain from the window.

Perfunctory rain had fallen in Wales and the West

Country. There had been showers in Scotland, a downpour in Northumbria. Over London and the south-east
thunder rumbled and the sky darkened. At the first drops
of rain householders stepped grinning into the streets,
waving to one another and presenting their palms to the
heavens like Indians greeting the monsoons. Miriam too,
having telephoned Scotland Yard to say Henry had
migraine and would be working from home, went into
the street and smiled when a droplet smote her head. The
fool from No. 17 was in the road with an umbrella, per-
forming a Sioux rain dance while children gallivanted
round him. For three or four minutes the skies dribbled
insufficiently even to discolour the pavements. Then they
lightened, became blue and the sun burned like a coal.
On the one o'clock news a Water Board functionary with
a pebble in his mouth warned that not only did the
morning's rain not constitute an end to the drought but
that reserves at this moment in time were so low that
contingency plans for a more meaningful escalation of the
conservation measures already in force would have to be
implemented without delay if viability in industry and
agriculture were not to be stifled within the parameters of
what might fairly be termed a siege situation.

Peckover switched off the radio. 'Miriam?' He shuffled
from the bedroom. 'Miriam?'

She appeared at the foot of the stairs, buxom and
stunning as always, in Peckover's estimation, and whisking a frothy mixture in a bowl.

'Goodbye,' she said.

'What?'

'Goodbye then.'

'Ah, please. Only a couple of hours, love. See a man.
What's in the bowl?'

'Extract of poppy, cupful of asbestos. Are you thinking
of coming back?'

'What's that supposed to mean?'

She was already walking away.

'Look, the leg's all right! The head's all right! I'm all right, I tell you!'

She had gone.

'What're you on about!' Peckover shouted into the empty space at the foot of the stairs. 'So it's Sunday! I'm a policeman, not a shop assistant! Policemen, firemen, fishermen, bus conductors – okay?'

From the kitchen answered clinking noises.

His leg was grazed from hip to ankle but not yet ready for amputation. He hopped half way down the stairs and leaned over the banister. 'And bishops – d'you hear? Bishops and parsons!'

Peckover seethed and shaved. A Charlie he looked in the bandage which was no longer even white but grubby and patterned over the left temple with what seemed to be fuel oil. He found unripped, unpressed trousers and an unmatching jacket. He made three telephone calls, after the third of which he sat, listened, and found the house relentlessly silent. He knew he should seek out Miriam.

He checked his wallet, notebook and car keys and hobbled from the house.

The room overflowed with amplifiers and greenery. Palms, rubber plants, banana plants, spear-shaped vegetation like berserk aspidistras, ankle-encircling tendrils, stalks thick as your thigh and giant insect-breeding pineapple-tops sprouted from troughs and jardinières. They obliterated the light from the window, crept across the ceiling, filled the air with damp and chlorophyll, and harboured, Peckover was convinced, if not Tarzan at least baby alligators. Too late he wished he had waited until tomorrow when he might have bearded the former planning officer to East Middlesex Council not here in this suburban Sumatra but in his architect's office in central London. Better still, for all the progress he was making or

seemed likely to make, he should have mislaid both
addresses and bearded him never at all, anywhere. The
feudal chanting through the amplifiers was hushed.
Monteverdi, Palestrina, one of those. His host had turned
the record-player down but not off. Peckover would have
turned the former planning officer off and the music up.
Perhaps the greenery and alligators waxed only to the
hum of cathedral plainsong? Perhaps if the plainsong were
silenced the banana plant would reach out and throttle
Malcolm York. No bad thing either, Peckover considered.

'Listen, let me fill you in,' York was saying.

He was no Tarzan himself but the school swot, intense
behind spectacles, with spots on his chin and lank damp
hair. Peckover recalled with surprise that York was not
many years younger than himself, according to the Molehill file. He looked like the local Trotskyite candidate,
sexually retarded and doomed to lose his deposit.

'I'll fill you in. There are twenty-six thousand elected
local councillors in the UK. Seven million public employees. Know how much they spend on goods and services, how much passes through their hands – *per annum*?'

Peckover did not know. He raised with an effort a
questioning eyebrow.

'*Six thousand one hundred million.* Six thousand one
hundred million! All right, you're going to say, a drop in
the ocean when you set it beside the GNP. Listen, d'you
know how much on capital investment?'

Peckover shifted position in the comfortless chair. This
was worse than the Molehill file. What if the fellow were
to say, 'Guess?' Peckover raised a second eyebrow.

'Guess,' said York.

Peckover, shaking his head, inclined forward expect-
antly. He had forgotten the question.

'*Seven hundred million!* Another drop in the ocean? All
right, for argument's sake we'll accept your point of view.

But you're not going to tell me that a percentage of seven hundred millions of public money, I don't care if it's only oh-oh-oh-one per cent, you're not going to tell me a percentage of that isn't going to stick to someone's fingers somewhere along the line.'

'Greenmead's not all public money. Zadiq's Gulf Consortium – '

'Excuse me, we're not talking about Zadiq's Gulf Consortium. I'll get to the private sector in a minute. All right, you're going to tell me we have the most selfless, least corrupt public servants in the world. Possibly you're right. Frankly I'm not informed about the situation in Montenegro and Billings, Montana. What I'm saying is that corruption is secretive almost by definition, it's not something you do in the street. Nothing's harder to detect or prove. My opinion is you're wasting your time but it's not my business any more. Listen, I'll fill you in.'

A desire for a pub and a pint engulfed Peckover. What were the chances of a heart attack laying the man low? Nothing painful or permanent. Merely a temporary disablement. Enough to allow the tip of the hat, the murmured regret, the exit.

'Know how many of these seven million have been convicted under the Prevention of Corruption Acts in the past ten years? I'll tell you. One hundred and eighty-eight. *One hundred and eighty-eight out of seven million!*' The chanting through the amplifiers had come to a stop. York had begun pacing a section of carpet between two silent amplifiers. He paced with a stooping, energetic gait, head advancing and retracting like a goose's. 'That's not including police. Fifteen were local councillors. Another seventeen or eighteen were civil servants. The rest, local authority employees and nationalized industries. What does that tell you?'

'Police convictions wouldn't affect the figure much.'

'You miss the point. One hundred and eighty-eight out

of seven million is point oh-oh-oh-three per cent convictions. Either our public servants are virtually in-
corruptible, which is what we choose to believe, or there's
another factor.' He paced a different section of carpet,
goose-necked, ducking under fronds, hands cupped as if
weighing sugar. 'Might it be they're getting away with it,
some of them? If you're not detected you're not convicted – correct? And you're not detected either because
someone covers up or nothing can be proved. Suspicion,
yes – proof, no. That's what I choose to believe, Mr ah –
Inspector – and I happen to have had some experience.
How many Greenmeads are happening at this moment
throughout the country? Can you tell me that? Now, take
Poulson.'

'If we could get back – '

'Listen. Here we have the classic case of recent years,
one might say of this century. We're talking about Britain
not Billings, Montana, or Watergate – '

'I'd appreciate it if you'd leave Billings – '

'Please, in a moment. How many candidates for corruption were investigated in the Poulson affair? I'll tell
you. Three hundred. You accept three hundred? And
how many were tried and convicted?'

York vanished into the jungle. There fell a silence, then
a whirring and a click. Fronds stirred. An alligator's got
him, Peckover thought. Side two of the plainsong,
identical to side one, murmured through the amplifiers.
Fronds parted. York emerged like Dr Livingstone from
the undergrowth.

'Twelve! Twelve convictions out of three hundred
possible suspects! And why did the public prosecutor's
office abandon investigations? Because we have laws
prohibiting access to bank accounts. Because our police
are still forbidden to search a suspect's house or business
premises without – '

'I'm familiar with all this, Mr York. Would you tell me – '

'Talk. talk, endless talk about standards of conduct in public life, all we get is talk – '

'Who approached you with the offer of the planning job at East Middlesex?'

'What? Who approached me? Beeston, I suppose.'

'We've copies of the letters confirming the appointment. But the first approach, was that a letter?'

'I don't know. No, a phone call. Wicks. He was deputy chairman.'

'You told 'im you'd think about it?'

'Certainly. The sheer scale of Greenmead had immense possibilities. Have you seen the shopping precinct? But Westminster Council had offered me – '

'Then the letters?'

'The what?'

'After the phone call, the letters.'

'After the phone calls, the lunches.'

'Beeston?'

'Of course. Some fish restaurant – Bentley's? Simpson's twice. You've had all this. Some sergeant. And Mr Farnsworth. They took it all down.'

'Beeston gave you the overall picture, did 'e? Green-mead – Zadiq's application for the green belt?'

'First time at Simpson's he brought the preliminary plans. Impressive too, I admit it. The shopping – '

'Did 'e mention Mountain – or Zadiq?'

'Expect so. Must have.'

'Did you meet them, either of them?'

'Not then. Listen, I'll fill you in. Surely your fraud branch has all this? Fact was, no question, I didn't realize it but I was being softened up. They hoped.' York was pacing again, dodging greenery. 'Lunch, bait, promises, all the benefits beyond the salary. They wanted a planning officer who'd be a rubber stamp. I was the consultant they appointed – I'm not saying they didn't approach others but I'd something of a reputation, the laboratory extension at Keele, Truscott House in Liverpool, they're mine – and they appointed me because they believed I'd be the rubber stamp, and they believed I knew they believed it and would accept it.'

'Accept being a rubber stamp?'

'Yes, yes. You've had all this.'

'Bit naïve of you?'

'Totally. But the possibilities of Greenmead – can you guess the square footage of the shopping precinct as originally proposed? I'll tell you. From the north quadrant – '

'But you didn't accept it?'

'Accept what?'

'F'rinstance, you opposed the new contracts for the public sector going to Mountain's – '

'No vision. Soul of a plasterer. The son's worse. I'm not saying on the purely practical side – '

'And you opposed Zadiq's encroaching on the green belt?'

'Naturally. Let me fill you in. The acreage – '

'And you were such a pain generally to the crew who thought they 'ad a rubber stamp that they gave you an 'undred quid in oncers to see things their way.'

'I never touched it.'

'I'm aware of that.'

'They put it up to five hundred.'

'Then they sacked you.'

'Technically, no. A vote of no confidence. That's what happens when a council's all one way – Tory or Labour, doesn't matter. I resigned.'

'But you didn't shut up.'

'Listen, the whole country's spread with concrete muck thrown up for a fast profit and here was – '

'So you had a visit from Willie McLeod.'

'Who?'

'You 'eard.'

'No, no. Willie McLeod? No, don't know him.'

'You got a note warnin' you off.'

'You've had all this.'

'Then a visit from Willie McLeod.'

York stopped pacing to inspect a spout of fringed greenery. 'Possibly. Red hair, flattened nose. He never really introduced himself.' He moved to a stem bearing a single red blossom and positioned his own nose above the blossom. 'Bastards.'

'Rough you up at all?'

'No.'

No, he wouldn't need to, Peckover thought. First the bribes and if they didn't work, next the muscle, or in the case of York the threat of muscle. From backhander to uppercut. An effective pattern. York, Ross Carter, God knew how many more.

With himself they'd skipped the bribe. Straight into the heavy stuff. Why?

They'd hardly have run out of funds. Were they sick of paying out? Or did they know a straight copper from a bent copper simply by looking at him? The smile on his face and the light in his eyes? An honour when you thought about it, never to have been offered the hundred quid. You'd need psychology as well as cash and muscle if you were to make a go of the corruption game, and no denying the Greenmead lot were making a go of it.

He said, 'You don't by any chance 'ave a drink?'

'A drink?'

'Warm in 'ere. All these plants.'

'What sort of drink?'

'Never mind. Doesn't matter.' Peckover stood up and put on his hat. 'I can find my way, no need to see me out.'

He awaited the hostly contradiction and opening of the door. The architect did not appear to have heard. He was scrutinizing a frond as though in search of greenfly.

'Bastards,' York muttered as the policeman retreated from the room.

A head with a handlebar moustache protruded round the frosted-glass door of the fraud squad. The eyes above the moustache swivelled, taking in Sands, Milton, Harris peeling an orange, and Detective-Sergeant Terry Sutton. Inspector Veal's moustache had won first prize on the occasion he had been inveigled, one weekend leave, into a moustache competition on Brighton pier.

'Mr Peckover not in yet?' Veal said.

'Got migraine,' Sutton said.

'That was yesterday. Ask him to buzz me soon as he gets in. The DC wants to see him – eleven o'clock.'

'He's got the job?'

'What job?'

'Poet Laureate.'

'Very droll.'

'Droll? Ten quid a year and the crown of laurel leaves?'

'Crown you, Sergeant. Just watch it. Eleven o'clock, you tell him.'

Veal and his moustache withdrew. Milton resumed his telephone conversation with his mother, Sands assaulted his typewriter, Harris sucked his orange with a sound like the bursting of the Great Boulder Dam. Sergeant Sutton slid Molehill part two off Credit Cards (pt. 6 Metropolitan Area CC/TS/1FS Blue Confidential), whither he had slid it when the door had opened.

No joke, this racket. Start to win on bank thefts and the villains switched to something else. Hundred and forty-eight million quid's worth of loot nicked in Britain last year, every year the figure up and the rate of nicked credit cards and cheque books up faster than anything else. Nicked cheques were selling for a fiver each, Croydon

way. Six quid in the provinces. Sight more urgent than a
fistful of twisters in local government.

Terry Sutton, second row forward on the Metropolitan
Police B rugby team, was built and complexioned like a
snowy Alp. He doodled on his blotter, multiplying thirty
by thirty by – what? Up to thirty quid you could draw
on a cheque against a credit card. Thirty cheques to a
cheque book. How long to tour thirty banks, cashing one
cheque per bank? In London you'd do a bank every ten
minutes if you left your car at home. So five hours, nine-
thirty to three-thirty, the length of time the banks were
open. You'd have to skip lunch. Nine hundred quid for a
day's work, given a credit card, cheque book and a
passable knack at forging a signature. You could practise
the signature at breakfast. Four thousand quid for a five-
day week.

Quarter of a million in a year.

When Peckover walked in at 10.35 an urge surged in
Sutton to stand and cry, 'Quarter of a million a year! You
want me to keep at it or drop it all for bloomin' Beeston!'

'Mornin',' Peckover grunted and hung up his hat. He
was unsmiling under the stormcloud of bandage.

Milton muttered into the telephone and replaced it.
Harris secreted a half-sucked orange behind *Criminal Law*,
vol II. Sutton slid Molehill over Credit Cards.

Peckover sat at his desk, took from an inside pocket an
oblong envelope and placed it in front of him.

'Sergeant?'

Sergeant Sutton sprinted.

'One, I want Willie McLeod finding.' Peckover rum-
maged in a drawer. 'You don't bring 'im in, you don't
even speak to 'im, you just find out where 'e is. Two,
Zadiq, same thing, and if 'e's round the far side of the
world, when's 'e contemplating coming back? Three,
Beeston. What's the matter?'

'Could I just get a pencil, sir?'

'Three, Beeston, see 'im. That watch, BB with love and
kisses, 'e's told Long it's not 'is, 'e's never seen it. I say
'e's lying and either Dawn de Nuit pinched it or 'e forgot
it in 'is excitement. If Zadiq was a customer, why not
Beeston? All pals together. So lean as 'ard as you like.
Four – '

'Could I take the watch along, sir?'

'Course you can't take the watch along. Long's got it.
If you can get it from 'im you're a better man than I take
you for. Four – God, now what's the matter?'

Sutton was looking at the watch on his wrist. 'Sorry.
Before I forget. Would you phone Inspector Veal? The
DC wants to see you at eleven.'

'The DC?' Peckover pulled at an earlobe. 'What're you
three staring at then!' he shouted across the office.

Sands, Milton and Harris hurled themselves at papers
and ledgers.

'Sir, sorry, one other thing. That watch. I've been going
through the file – '

'Makes a change.'

'Yes sir – that's to say, August twelfth, nineteen seventy-
five, on the back of the watch. You'll have spotted it yourself, naturally, it's the day the planning committee
awarded the first contract on the Greenmead development. For the council offices and library.'

'Oh?'

'Sir.'

'To Thomas Mountain and Son?'

'Right.'

'That so? A wee giftie from Mountain to Beeston for
services rendered. Good. Very good. In that case – four,
see Mountain too. Lean on the father, don't lean on the
son, he might bruise then we'll all be up the creek. Five,
get 'old of Long. I want the latest on the girl.'

Peckover opened a drawer which was empty except for
one unused fraud-issue calculator. He slammed the

drawer shut, opened another and resumed rummaging.
'Six, Ames-Clegg, 'e's in the south of France, I want the
day and hour 'e's expected back. Phone 'is 'Exham place.
If that's shut up find the secretary. Reasonable politeness,
Sergeant. Seven, Rifty. She's on 'oliday too, so same thing
without the politeness – '

'Rifty?'

'Rift, man. Olympia Rift. Queen of Tarts. Vice'll give
you – '

'Sorry, sir. What's her real name?'

'That is 'er real name, dammit. If she wasn't rich as
flamin' Crœsus already she'd not 'ave taken off in the
tourist season. Eight – '

Eight hung unspoken in the air. Peckover slid the rum-
maged drawer shut and regarded a blank area of white-
emulsion wall. Sutton wrote hard, catching up with five,
six and seven.

'Eight,' Peckover said, opening the right-hand drawer
and plucking out a brown OHMS envelope. He drew
towards him the oblong envelope which he had brought
into the office. 'Take this to Veal. It's our first backhander.'

'How much?' Sutton heard himself say.

Peckover wrote on the OHMS envelope, *For Attention,
Deputy Commander (Crime), New Scotland Yard.*

'Two-fifty,' he said and tapped the oblong envelope.
'Count it. Then you can sign this.'

The stamp on the oblong envelope had been franked on
Saturday, 11.15 a.m., in London SW1. The penmanship
might have been an infant's except that the spelling was
correct. Either that or it had been written backwards or
with the pen held between the teeth. *Personal and Private
Henry Peckover Esq., 32 Collins Cross, London NW1.* While
Sutton counted, Peckover wrote a memo to the deputy
commander.

'No note, sir?'

'What d'you expect – "Get well soon"?' He looked up, staring again at the blank wall. 'Phone call though, 'alf hour after the post came. Asked if I'd received my honorarium, said Greenmead was a waste of my valuable time and there'd be the same again following evidence of my good faith.'

'Beeston?'

'Dunno. Don't think so. Alderman's language, though.'

'One of the Mountains?'

'Told you, I don't know. He 'ung up.'

In curt sentences the memorandum noted the bribe and telephone call. Both policemen signed. Peckover put the memorandum and envelope of banknotes into the brown envelope, sealed it and handed it to Sutton.

'Excuse me, sir, if you're seeing the DC at eleven –'

'Get it to Veal, lad.'

Peckover pushed back his chair. He collected his hat and walked from the office. Sutton stroked his chin with the envelope.

Harris said, 'That the protocol, is it – you wear a hat for the DC?'

'It's part of the ceremony,' Sands explained. 'You go in wearing the hat and you come out wearing the laurel crown.'

'If you go in,' murmured Sutton.

CHAPTER VIII

PC Armitage paced in a northerly direction along the east side of Smith Square. Here was posh parliamentary territory, residential, and in the estimation of PC Armitage, achingly boring.

Boring but risky. You were on a hiding to nothing.

Nothing happened in this acre of Westminster, not at

three o'clock in the morning with Parliament in recess and
the residents either touring the Greek Islands or, if in some
borrowed castle in the Highlands, writing their memoirs.
No punch-ups, race riots, boozed football crowds.
Occasionally a boozed MP but they were best helped or
ignored, not messed with, unless you had a dozen witnesses. In fifteen minutes there had been one taxi and not
one pedestrian. On the other hand, if anything did happen
it was likely to be too much for one copper on his own and
no question of glory, or not in this world. Like a lunatic
with a bomb. It had happened. The nearness of the Yard
was no consolation when a row of fancy houses blew up
and the limbs of cabinet ministers circled through the air.

Invisibly beyond the rooftops, a hundred yards north-
west, lay Scotland Yard; a hundred yards north-east, the
Houses of Parliament; a hundred yards directly north,
Westminster Abbey. PC Armitage trod from Smith
Square into Lord North Street and paused. Diagonally
across the road something had moved.

No one was in the street apart from himself. He looked
back, then across the road again to the street-level window
where something, he believed, had moved. Already he was
beginning to doubt. Why anyway should something not
move? The Lord Chancellor, sleepless and hunting for
cornflakes? A ladyship's cat prowling the chintz? Keeping his eyes on the window, PC Armitage walked past the
house of Sir Cyril Ames-Clegg. Then he crossed the road.

The window was so dark he could not at first tell
whether there were drawn curtains, lace, a blind or
nothing at all. Eventually he made out through the glass
and parted curtains an outline of furniture. He moved to
his left and tried the brass handle of the door. He twisted it
both ways, shoulder against the door.

Under a street lamp he took out a notebook and flipped
the pages. Here it was, he'd thought so, family away until
the sixth, house to be watched. Like fifty others. Some of

this lot thought they ought to have a Grenadier guards-
man on the doorstep every time they waltzed off to the
Riviera. PC Armitage stepped backwards into the road
and stood for a full minute, observing the house.

He crossed to the opposite pavement and walked on,
regarding a window here, a basement area there. He
turned into Cowley Street. All the same he'd return in
ten minutes. Five minutes, he decided.

Inside the room, after the last footsteps had faded, a man
in pink kitchen gloves counted to fifty. Then he groped
along the wall, round a dresser with propped plates and
back into the hall. Another scare like that he'd deluge his
trousers.

Nowhere was darker than the narrow hall. By touch he
found the door opposite and entered a room dimly
illumined by the light from the street. There were armchairs, roll-top desk, a bookcase, photographs on the
mantelpiece, a cabinet, an ineradicable cigar-smell. Why
didn't the buggers draw the curtains before they swanned
off? He could leave them undrawn and risk being spotted
from the street or draw them and risk the curiosity of an
ambitious constable.

How long before the man on the beat would be back?
Half an hour? He edged to the window and looked out
from the side. He ducked, crawled beneath the window
and looked out from the other side. He drew the curtains,
then pressed the nipple of his torch.

In two strides he reached the cabinet and opened it.
Within stood a supermarket of bottles.

Well, many an instance there'd been of a burglar found
unconscious on the carpet with the whisky bottle. In his
case it looked like being the rum bottle. Rum was not
normally his tipple, too smelly, but the whiskies and
brandies were full-size. The rum bottle was half-size and
flat. He unscrewed the cap, took a substantial swig,
gasped and screwed on the cap. He slid the bottle into

his jacket pocket. Blame the butler. Probably wouldn't even be missed among these glass battalions. Keeping the beam low, he pointed the new Woolworth's torch at the legs of furniture. The beam moved up a cube of green steel beside the desk and rested on the disc covering the keyhole.

It was to have been expected. Damn and damn anyway. The safe was an antique but he'd never pick it and no future in trying. So much for taking the putrid law into your own hands. Anything incriminating and either it would be locked in Swiss bank accounts or in this damn safe.

So his breaking-in was not only criminal but futile. He needed his mind examining. But he had never asked to be a policeman, never asked for the fraud branch and Molehill. How the hell else did you put away rich villains who had your skull cracked open simply by lifting the phone and dialling the right number? What kind of country where fat profiteers bought their way round the law and policemen were slugged?

Peckover sat at the desk, slid the roll-top up and started investigating at speed the side drawers, left hand foraging, right hand training the torch. All was neatness: paperclips, sealing wax, stamps, stationery. There might be keys. This would not be the first householder with a locked safe and the key twelve inches away.

There were four keys. He tucked the disc to one side and tried each in turn in the keyhole of the safe. None fitted. He returned them to the drawer, slid the roll-top down and went through the deep drawers in the pedestal legs: boxes of filched House of Commons notepaper, folders of correspondence labelled Constituency, folders of insurance, domestic bills, television and gun licences, a riding-crop, a cricket ball, photographs of cricket teams with his nibs youthful in white, photographs of his nibs on horseback, a photograph showing him in tweeds with a double-barrelled shotgun standing astride a mound of what looked like chickens, boxes of horsey medallions and rosettes, indiscriminate rubbish. But no more keys. Apart from keys to the safe he did not even know what he was looking for. In the bottom drawer in the right-hand pedestal, beneath tidy college and regimental scarves, he found a cylindrical box of Ali Izmir Turkish Delight.

The box lay unopened in its Cellophane skin. Peckover picked up the box. As well be hanged for a sheep as a lamb, he supposed. The box was too fat to fit in his jacket pocket, even the pocket which did not hold the rum. He should've brought a swag bag, he thought. He unbuttoned his shirt, slipped the box inside and buttoned the shirt over it. A bright story for Mr Ross Carter this one would make – Scotland Yard Inspector on Burglary Charge. 'I Only Took Rum And Turkish Delight, They Were Going Off Anyway.' How long had he wasted at the desk? Ten minutes? There was still upstairs.

Peckover listened. His head was hot beneath the off-white bandages, his neck clammy from the heat of a navy woollen scarf. Apart from his own breathing there was only stillness, silence.

He swigged from the rum bottle. Demon rum, how would we manage without you? He would have liked to know. He positioned the chair against the desk and followed the beam of his torch into the hall. On the walls were hunting scenes. To the left the stairs, to the right the street door, and in a wire cage beneath the brass letter-slit an accumulation of mail. He trod along the hall and dipped a rubber-gloved hand into the cage.

Squatting, torch on the carpet, he held the mail in the beam and sifted through periodicals, publicity, coupons for twopence off everything, brown envelopes with see-through windows, white envelopes addressed in long-hand and envelopes from overseas with blue and red borders. He reached up, dropping item by worthless item back into the cage. He was about to reach up with a plump white envelope when the postmark caught his eye.

Sat 11.15 a.m. London SW1.

He thumbed open the envelope and peered in at a wad of banknotes: mauvish, bound in a band of brown paper and decorated with St George, Britannia, Queen Elizabeth II and Shakespeare, chin on hand, leaning with an abstracted air.

No letter that he could see. Peckover on his haunches stared beyond the ripped rim of the envelope at an area of skirting-board. What the devil did he do now? Drop it back in the cage and trust the butler might be held responsible along with the rum and Turkish Delight? If he held on to it, how explain at the Yard how it came into his hands?

Slipped to him by a man in the street, an informer, name and address unknown? Dropped on the pavement by the postman?

Because here at last was something. Saturday at 11.15 a.m. in London SW1 had been pay parade in Greenmead circles. Explanations could be dreamed up later.

Peckover put the envelope with the banknotes into his breast pocket. The next letter, also addressed to Sir Cyril Ames-Clegg, MP, had a blue and red border and an impressive origin: Crédit Suisse, Paradeplatz 8, CH–8021, Zürich, Switzerland. Peckover added it to the pay parade envelope.

The origin of the next was the National Trust, addressed to Lady Millicent Ames-Clegg. Peckover, reaching up to the wire cage, saw the brass door handle turn.

For what seemed to him an unconscionable passage of time he was incapable of movement. He could not even release the National Trust letter into the cage. He watched the bulbous brass twist to the right, to the left, and listened to the rasp of each twist. Then he listened to one, two, three, four blasts of a police whistle from the other side of the door. He was slow, he had even begun to wonder where he was and why the whistling? Only at the fifth blast did he find himself dashing along the hall.

In the kitchen his knee sent a chair skeetering across the floor. He climbed into the sink, pushed open the window he had left ajar and scrambled through. He fell among broad beans. His torch he crammed into the jacket pocket which was free of rum; the navy woollen scarf he wrapped over the bandage and tied under his chin. The jacket bagged, the scarf tickled his ears. He looked like a countrywoman in winter.

There came a shout, not close. Peckover stumbled through rose-bushes and darkness to the end of the garden and put his hands over the wall. He hauled himself up. Wooden trellis snapped under his shoes.

Which way? Either way, Smith Square or back into Great Peter Street, he'd find police unless he spurted. Precariously balanced he trod left and into the branches of an apple tree. He forced his way through. A branch rebounded and whipped the side of his head.

'Cover Peter Street!' a voice called, this time not far distant.

Ape-like through ivy and dark Peckover trod in a rapid crouch. If he fell, would he fall into garden statuary? A glasshouse? He teetered and clung with both hands to ivy-matted wall as a shape came cat-screeching from nowhere and disappeared into nowhere. At the wall's end, with barely a glance at the helmeted blue figure advancing beneath the lamps along the north of the street, he dropped backwards to the pavement and fell on his side. He heard glass crunch beneath him, then a shout and a whistle-blast.

Peckover raced for the gloom of Dean Trench Street, away from the policeman and almost into the arms of a second policeman. Like the cat, the second policeman had arrived from nowhere. Peckover ducked his head and kept going. His skull cracked into the policeman's cheek, his shoulder barged the reeling blue barrier aside.

He sprinted into Tufton Street, across Horseferry Road and south towards Pimlico. Running, he listened for shouts and whistles. He heard none; only his own slapping shoes and panting. His leg hurt, and his head. If the copper had recognized him he was done, he as well might save his breath, sit in the road and wait for them. He ran harder, grunting and wheezing.

He kept running, a square countrywoman with slapping feet and a wet side, into the warrens of Pimlico, pursued at each stride by a reek of rum.

Sunshine sloped in at the door of the foreman's hut. Alderman Beeston said, 'It'll be all right. He's fixed. If he was straight we'd have heard about it.'

'Cloud-cuckoo land, you,' grumbled Thomas Mountain. He wiped a handkerchief round the inside of his collar. 'We're the ones are going to be fixed. Fixed for seven years in the Scrubs.'

'I agree with Basil – ' Rupert Mountain said.

'No one asked you,' said the father.

'Two-fifty's as good as a month's wage for that one,' Rupert insisted. 'Not that I'm saying it won't cost us another two-fifty before we're out of the wood.'

'Add a nought, I'm with you,' said the father.

'Balls,' said Beeston. 'What you lack is psychology, Thomas. They're all bent, the knack is pricing them, like Zadiq's always saying. Mind you, if you've got Zadiq's bank account you price high and win every time.'

'Don't mention that bugger's name to me.'

'More phone calls?'

'Two nights ago from Toronto. Half past four. Said he knew who was blackmailing him and unless the gentleman found a stone to hide under he was going to be cut in two.' Mountain puffed out round clammy cheeks. 'Don't know why he told me.'

'He told me too,' Beeston said. 'Six o'clock. It's his way
of discouraging imitators.'

Alderman and builder looked at each other and at
troubled Rupert, then at each other again.

'Suppose he didn't mention who?' Mountain said.

'Not to me.'

Rupert Mountain mashed out his cigarette under his
shoe and lit another. 'Somebody's going to cut Zadiq in
two one of these days.'

The father said, 'Don't approve of the physical stuff,
never did and never will, but I'll tell you this. If any
blackmailer gets it, that's all right with me.'

'All I'm saying is the copper's fixed,' Beeston said. 'It's
going to be all right.'

'All I'm saying is I don't like it,' said Thomas Mountain.

'He'll like it. Two-fifty? All right, call it five by the time
he cries off.' Beeston swatted his hand in front of his face,
dispersing cigarette smoke. 'God's sake, what is he? A
poor pathetic policeman and a poet. I'm a monkey's
uncle if he gets more than a tenner a poem.'

'A poet?' Mountain mopped his pate. 'Queer, is he?'

The son put on his white helmet. 'I've got to collect the
invoices for the steel,' he said.

'They'll keep, I won't,' said a blond giant walking
into the hut. 'Siddown. Won't take more than an hour or
day or two.'

'Not again,' breathed Thomas Mountain. 'You a
copper?'

'Sergeant Sutton,' Sergeant Sutton said, and closed the
door. 'Which is the one bruises easily?'

Squares of light as from a battery of slide-projectors
patterned the corridor wall where sunshine entered
through the windows. Detective-Inspector Peckover lifted
his knuckles to the door with the plaque, Deputy Com-

mander. Worse things 'ave 'appened at sea, he told himself. If 'e shoots it'll be between the eyes, you'll 'ardly feel
a thing.

'Enter.'

Peckover entered and closed the door.

'Sit down, Inspector.'

So, he was still an inspector.

The room was adequately pile-carpeted and the desk
behind which sat the deputy commander was no stores-
issue officers-for-the-use-of desk but a graceful prize,
more a table than a desk, which looked as though it
might have been rescued by dealers from a château about
the time of the French Revolution. On the wall one of the
prints bore more than a passing resemblance to a Hockney
swimming-pool. If it were not a print, Peckover decided,
advancing on the chair he presumed to be his, the DC
beyond further shadow of doubt was on the Greenmead
payroll too, because even on a DC's salary he'd not have
an original Hockney on his office wall. Apart from these
accessories and an understated uniform with a suggestion
of Savile Row, the man had what Peckover was sure were
good looks: small pleasant features of the Robert Redford
kind and a Curzon Street haircut. If there were an easy
way to come up, Peckover believed, the DC had come up
it. Public school, probably squash champion at Sandhurst.
Nothing so vulgar as boxing.

Off-centre in a chair at the side of the château-salvaged
desk sat Superintendent Adamson. The scene was not a
court-martial. Neither, on the other hand, was it sherry
and madeira cake. Peckover sat in a chrome and leather
chair diagonally across from the superintendent. The
leather sighed under him and he tested it discreetly for
movement. It swivelled, he discovered, but did not rock.
He believed he recognized one or two of the exhibits on
the tidy desk.

'Thought we were going to have a word yesterday at

eleven, Inspector. What happened?'

'Complete misunderstanding, sir. Entirely my fault. I understood it was to have been today.'

'How did that occur?'

'Error in communications, sir. I can only suppose I misheard.'

'I see.' The DC's chair both swivelled and rocked. Having swivelled to face Peckover, he now rocked backwards and forwards. 'Well, no harm. I hope. How's the head?'

'Fine, thank you sir.'

'Good. Right then. First, our enquiry into part five of your Greenmead Development file. I'm told it went astray in the reshuffle.' He leaned forward, picked up a folder, dropped it on the desk in front of Peckover and leaned back. 'Enquiries sometimes have a way of producing results even before they get started, Inspector. You were absolutely right to be worried. It was in C-Nine among some lab reports.'

'Might I ask who discovered it, sir?'

'Who discovered it, Ted?'

'Believe it was Sergeant Wallace, sir,' said the superintendent.

'File it with the others, Inspector.' The DC, rocking, fixed frank Robert Redford eyes on Peckover. 'In fact it's of no further interest to you personally. I'm taking you off Greenmead.'

He waited for Peckover's reply. Peckover remained silent.

'You're too high a risk,' said the DC. 'What's going on?'

'Don't quite understand, sir.'

'I suspect you do. I'm not objecting to your being a risk to yourself, we can live with that. But without being pompous, we've the reputation of the force to consider. Where were you last night?'

'At home, sir.'

'With, ah – ' his eyes lowered, his forefinger ranged down a typed sheet of foolscap – 'Miss Turnbull, is it? Collins Cross?'

'Correct, sir.'

'Because there was a break-in at a house in Lord North Street. The MP, Ames-Clegg. Believe he crops up in the Greenmead file. Know anything about that?'

'About Ames-Clegg?'

'The break-in.'

'First I've 'eard of it, sir.'

'And last Saturday night?'

'Saturday night what, sir?'

'Sunday morning, to be exact. Around three o'clock.'

'Sunday morning three o'clock.' Peckover pondered. He plucked at an earlobe. 'Bed, sir. The 'ead was acting up a bit.'

'There were complaints of a disturbance in Ensign Terrace. You know Ensign Terrace?'

'Can't say I do, sir.'

'Registration of one of two cars involved was the same as your own car, Inspector. A Cortina, isn't it?' The fingers found another typed sheet. 'The letters of the registration, that is. Unfortunately they didn't get the figures. Or perhaps fortunately.'

'Not my car, sir. I can say that categorically.'

'Quite. I've decided not to pursue these matters, Inspector. Not for the moment anyway.' Hands clasped in his lap, the DC gently rocked. 'But you'll appreciate we can risk no more of it. It's not to be tolerated. Not if one of our own men is involved.'

'I don't follow what – '

'Your record is sound, Inspector. You're reliable, experienced, unfailingly honest – backbone of the police.' The fingers had picked up the plump envelope of pay parade money. Peckover glimpsed his own name and address in longhand. The envelope dropped back on the desk. 'You'll appreciate if there'd been the least suggestion of dishonesty I wouldn't hesitate. As it is, that bump on the head, I suspect you may not have fully recovered. Would you kick up if I suggested a spell of leave and a return to uniform?'

'With respect, sir, I believe I'm getting somewhere on the Greenmead business. There's a tie-in with the call-girl, Dawn de Nuit. I've not 'ad a chance to see Zadiq yet. I need more time but p'raps not too much more. If someone wasn't worried I'd not be getting coshed and bribed. I think I should keep with it.'

'I'm afraid I don't. Possibly it's a matter for the doctor.' The DC rocked back and held the backward position, fingertips together, eyes levelled at Peckover. 'To be frank, I've not made up my mind whether you should stay or transfer but I shall have by the time you're back from leave. How much leave has Inspector Peckover to come, Ted?'

'Week at least, sir,' replied the robot superintendent as if a penny had been dropped into the slot. 'Nearer two, counting days owed.'

'I don't want you going off abroad either, or to relations or staying in London. Total rest.' The DC was rocking again. 'I suppose you don't have a country cottage?'

'I suppose I don't. That's to say, no, sir.'

Reflecting, the DC pressed his fingertips to his temples. 'Borrow mine. We'll not be using it before the end of August. Couple of miles from Malmesbury. Does it appeal?'

'Very generous, sir, but I don't – '

'Would Miss Turnbull be able to go with you?'

'Really couldn't say, sir. I honestly don't – '

'Unless you've anything better to propose I think that's settled. I'll draw you a map. Key's in the watering-can in the shed. I want you off right away, Inspector. Out of it.

By tonight. London's become too treacherous for you.'

'Have to be at the hospital tomorrow, sir. The stitches come out.'

'What time?'

'Nine o'clock.'

'Immediately after the hospital, then. What're you doing this evening?'

'Couple of contacts, sir.'

'No contacts, Peckover. Nothing. You're staying in. You'll telephone Superintendent Adamson at eight, ten and twelve. Understand?'

'Sir.'

'For the time being you pass all the Greenmead papers to Sergeant Sutton. You realize you're being let off every kind of serious trouble, Inspector. In return I ask good behaviour. I demand it.'

'Sir.'

'I'll send up the map. D'you know Wiltshire?'

'No, sir.'

'My safety-valve. I envy you. Take a good pair of walking shoes. And a book or two on birds, wild flowers. You'll be surprised.'

The DC was rocking vigorously, lost in nostalgia, Peckover guessed, for wild flowers and countryside. If he tells me it's perfect for poetry I'll tell him not to be a patronizing bugger, I swear I will, Peckover thought.

'Might even find your muse serves you well, Inspector. I'd be delighted to see the results.'

'Thank you, sir.'

CHAPTER IX

'So the Irishman said, "No parking, no parking",' said Terry Sutton, and hugely grinning he lifted his pint to his lips.

'*Pom* pom pom *pom* pom, roses and lilies,' Peckover sang in a mumble, 'up your English country garden-O.'

' "No parking, no parking" – get it? See, he'd said the double – '

'Get it, get it. Very, very good, lad. Seriously. 'Eard it but it bears the retelling. Indeed yes. So you've nothing on wild flowers?'

'Sorry, sir.'

'Birds?'

'Something in the library, I expect.'

''Ow about walking shoes?'

'Be a bit big, sir.'

'Possibly. All yours, son.'

'Sir?'

'Molehill, lad. All yours.'

'Yes, sir, so you said. Do my best with it. There are one or two points have come up. I'd like your advice.'

'Why?'

'Well, naturally. Would you like to hear what I've got so far?'

'No. *Pom* pom pom *pom* pom, roses and lilies.' Mumbling, Peckover tapped his glass in rhythm. 'Whassa time?'

A quarter to three. The lunch-hour crowd had gone. Only the self-employed, unemployed and policemen put out to grass remained in the Fox and Goose. Peckover had started in the William IV, moved on to the Ship, then telephoned Sutton and commanded his presence.

As company. Not to listen to Molehill.

At the far end of the bar the barmaid knitted while discussing the cost of living with a man in a bowler hat. The landlord drifted between tables, gathering glasses.

'Go on then, lad. But under protest. I'm on leave.'

'Yes, sir. Some successes, some failures. I'll take them in order.' Sutton glanced round. He produced an envelope and a notebook. From the envelope he took photographs which he placed on the counter by Peckover's glass. 'One, Willie McLeod.'

A man posed in a crouch, fists raised, peered up from the top photograph. He had the obligatory squashed nose and what appeared to be freckles. Peckover slid the photograph aside with a finger to reveal a second photograph, then a third, both of the same freckled man in much the same crouch. He wore shorts and boxing gloves.

''E's a southpaw,' Peckover said.

'Light-heavyweight, sir, or he was then. More of an overweight these days, I wouldn't wonder. These were when he turned pro after the Tokyo Olympics. He was knocked out by a Roumanian in the quarter-finals. Kutchuk or someone. Remember?'

''Course I don't bloody remember. What d'you think I am, the *Sporting Dictionary*?'

Sutton, frowning, found a page in the notebook. 'Six years a professional, won twenty-eight, lost thirty-nine. Don't know whether it's significant but he lost four on fouls. Threw it in eighteen months ago, painter and decorator by trade, address – Four, Willoughby Grove, Tooting. Except he cleared out last month.'

'Pay the rent?'

'Yes, sir. No forwarding address.'

Peckover shuffled the photographs like a three-card trick. 'I'll 'ang on to this for the family album,' he said, picking a photograph at random and slotting it into his wallet. 'Drink up, lad. Time for another.'

'My round, sir.'

'Dead right. That the lot, then?'

'No, sir. Two, Zadiq. He probably left Dubai yesterday, possibly for New York. His Gulf Consortium are cagey, or just as likely they don't know. Can't we get Interpol on to him?'

''Ow? What's 'e done?'

'What about the call-girl? We could fudge up something.'

'You want to start an international oil embargo, lad, that's what you want. Another quid on petrol and a three-day week.'

'What I'd really like, speaking personally, would be a two-day week.'

'With you there, Sergeant. Next?'

'I saw Beeston and the Mountains. I'll come back to them in a moment. Quite a development there. Saw Long too. He didn't brim with information but Beeston was at a dance the night the girl was killed. Gangs of witnesses and no chance he could have been anywhere near Rydal Street. If he forgot his watch or she pinched it, it wasn't then.'

Peckover muttered into his latest pint, watching the froth. Sutton passed coins to the barmaid. She held her knitting under her arm.

'Ames-Clegg's due back Saturday. Whether the break-in'll bring him back sooner I wouldn't know.' Sutton risked a sidelong glance at the inspector, who was watching froth. He returned to the notebook. 'Rifty, no one seems to know. Last heard of with a German girl and a Lamborghini in Barcelona.'

'Olé,' Peckover said to the froth.

'Eight, I took the two-fifty to Veal. I don't know whether he passed it on to the DC.'

''E did. And while you're playing at cashiers, 'ere's

some more.' Peckover slid along the counter the envelope, now sealed inside a second envelope, looted from Sir Cyril Ames-Clegg's letter-box. 'Five 'undred and don't ask questions. I've not thought up the answers yet. Call it an interception. Lock it in my desk till I get back from the English country gardens.' He recovered the envelope and wrote on it, *For Attention, DS Sutton, Fraud Branch*, and signed his name. 'Second thoughts, lock it in your own desk. I might not 'ave a desk when I get back.'

'Time, gentlemen!' called the landlord.

Sutton stowed the envelope in his pocket. 'There's more to come, sir, I mean looks like there could be. When I saw the Mountains and Beeston. This is what I'd like your advice on. Have to admit, I don't care for all this – '

'*Pom* pom pom *pom* pom, something sweet Willies. Get to the point, lad. 'Ow much?'

'How much what?'

''Ow much more they coming up with?'

'Same again, sir. Two-fifty. If we lay off.'

'You didn't thump 'im, I 'ope? The young one.'

'Didn't lay a finger. Didn't have to. But there was a sort of hint if we didn't lay off there'd be no more, there'd be something else.'

'Like what?'

'That's what I asked. He wouldn't specify.'

'Which of 'em wouldn't specify?'

'The young one – Rupert.'

''E did the 'inting too?'

'Right.'

'You should've thumped 'im.'

'Damn sight sooner thump him than collect. What do we do, sir? I'm joking, all this folding stuff flapping about gives me the shakes. Like we're being set up.'

'They delivering or are you supposed to collect?'

'I collect at Mountain's house.'

'We're being set up. Insuring their old age with 'idden cameras and tapes and a shorthand writer under the bed. They must think we're amateurs.' Peckover gulped beer and wiped his mouth. 'Collect, lad. Tell Sands first. Write it down for 'im, the bugger's deaf far as I can make out. Then get it back to Veal or Adamson or anyone toute-de-suite before your pocket's picked. The more back-handers, the more the judge is going to lay on them. If it gets that far.'

'Time gentlemen, please!' the landlord sang.

'Give you a ring tonight, sir, if you're in.'

'I'm in. Confined to barracks. But don't ring. I might be round at the local.'

The Bull off Clapham Avenue South was plenty of people's local, though not Peckover's. Neither was it the first pub during the drought to have run out of lager, keg and draught beer. Peckover drank something gaseous poured from a bottle, then walked along the side of the Common towards the telephone-box.

Eight o'clock near enough. He dialled and pressed in the two-penny piece before anyone could have time to answer. If no one answered, there was a gone two pence he'd have problems explaining away on expenses. A woman's voice answered.

'. . . Yes, hello. Name's Peckover, Inspector Peckover. Might I 'ave a word with Superintendent Adamson? . . . Oh, sorry . . . No, no, don't disturb 'im. Would you mind telling 'im I'm at 'ome but I might slip out for a pint, no point him phoning me. I'll phone again at ten . . . Thanks, much obliged . . . Peckover, that's it. Goodbye.'

He crossed the road and walked along the pavement. On the Common dogs raced after flung sticks, youths kicked footballs. The evening was clammy. Distantly rumbled thunder which fooled nobody.

In the front garden of the Edwardian semi-detached

the queue of rose-trees flourished redly. Touch of sur-
reptitious watering in the small hours, Peckover suspected; by the wife while the Co-ordinator (Metropolitan
Area), Community Relations was out quelling a riot. He
remembered the bell; not a ring but a buzz. Could a bell
buzz? He pressed it.

She was less dishevelled than the previous time and even
more lissom in magenta slacks, a sleeveless blouse with
spangles across the pocket, and sandals which consisted of
a sole and a single magic thong round the big toe.

'Mr Peckover, isn't it? Hello. I'm afraid my husband's
out.'

'I know. I wondered if I might 'ave a word with you.
Won't take a minute.'

'With me?'

'Mind if I come in?'

She stood aside. Peckover entered with what he supposed could be described only as a sinking feeling.
Bridges burned, the Rubicon crossed, another nail in the
coffin. How many wrong decisions made up a lifetime?
In the sitting-room boomed massed strings, trombones
and trumpets. He spotted the uncapped gin bottle, ice and
tonics on the sideboard, and on the arm of a chair her
glass.

Olive Farnsworth switched off the record-player. 'Sit
down, do. How d'you mean, you knew he was out?'

'I'll not keep you. Quite unofficial. Just passing, really.'

'Like before.'

'Pardon?'

'A drink? You can have a drink if you're unofficial,
can't you?'

'I won't, no, thanks.'

'Scotch, wasn't it?'

'A smallish one. I'll get to the point, Mrs Farnsworth.
Slightly tricky.'

Like the magenta backside aimed at him from the

cabinet at which she stooped, collecting scotch and a glass. If she had not been aware just how tricky and trim her backside was she would not, Peckover believed, have been aiming it but angling it to one side. He looked away at the coffee-table heaped with magazines, the uniform book club editions in the bookcase, the middle-price furniture which might or might not have been bought out of middle-range backhanders. Nothing here beyond the range of a chief superintendent's salary.

'I took over a file when your 'usband was promoted and there were gaps. Nothing important, one or two minor bits missing. Sometimes 'appens in a reshuffle. No question of blame, nothing like that, but I 'esitate to approach your 'usband directly.' And that was the day's understatement. Peckover watched her pouring whisky. He had seen hands which were steadier. 'You'll agree 'e's a most sensitive and capable man, 'e just might misinterpret. You could probably fill in a couple of gaps yourself.'

'Water or soda, Inspector?'

'Drop of water, thanks. Like, f'rinstance, d'you remember had your 'usband entertained an MP 'ere – Sir Cyril Ames-Clegg? Mean, no reason why not, your 'usband's contacts, socially and professionally – '

'I disgraced myself. The rice was burnt and the lamb raw. Or the other way round. Another memorable evening for the Farnsworths of Clapham.'

'Sorry.'

'Which disgraced Gerry too, of course. Not for the first time. He wasn't thrilled.'

''Ow long ago was this?'

'Year? Really can't remember. Chin-chin.'

Bottoms up, Peckover was tempted to say. She had seated herself low down in the armchair opposite, almost sprawled, beslacked legs crossed at the knee, hand on the armrest holding a refreshed gin. His smallish whisky failed by a quarter of an inch to reach the rim of the glass.

It tasted unwatered.

'Just the once, was it?'

'The burnt rice or the MP?'

'Ames-Clegg.'

'It's always just the once, Inspector. We don't seem to entertain a great deal these days. Am I allowed to call you Henry?'

Peckover mumbled.

'I've a feeling Gerry lunches people in town. And is lunched, I suppose. He doesn't bring people home any more. Why d'you think that should be, Henry?'

The voice if not the words held more than a hint of mockery. Peckover mumbled again, swigged discreetly and coughed. Mrs Farnsworth put her ginless hand behind her head and rested it there, directing at the inspector a nude armpit.

'You married, Henry?'

'In a way.'

'In a way? I like "in a way". Children?'

'No. If you don't mind, Mrs Farnsworth.' He emitted a brisk clearing of the throat. 'So although Ames-Clegg 'asn't been 'ere for a year it's possible they meet in town.'

'More than likely. Has he done anything wrong?'

'Who?'

'How d'you mean?'

'You said, "Has 'e done anything wrong?" I said, "Who?" '

'I meant Sir Cyril but either of them if you like. Honestly, Henry, this conversation gets more and more weird.' Her hand supported the back of her head, the armpit pointed with the subtlety of a missile launcher. 'Call me Olive.'

'Mm. Would your 'usband's relations with Ames-Clegg be more social or professional, would y' say?'

'Oh, professional. Mine are social.'

'I don't quite follow.'

'I'm sure you do.'

Peckover wished he had stayed at home. From a jacket pocket he brought out the cylindrical box of Ali Izmir Turkish Delight. 'Are these familiar to you?'

'What are they – exhibit number one?'

He waited, holding the box on view like an auctioneer.

'A present?' Olive Farnsworth giggled and sipped. 'Henry, you shouldn't have.'

'Does your 'usband by any chance 'ave a sweet tooth, Mrs Farnsworth, or is it just you?'

'Gerry has a sweet nothing.' The foot of her crossed leg rocked rhythmically, the sandal dangling from its magic toe-thong. 'Offer me one, then.'

'Can you remember about Ames-Clegg the evening 'e was 'ere? Did you offer Turkish Delight?'

'Heavens, how do I know? You ask the weirdest questions.'

'Or After Eights or those chocolate things like sticks? You'll remember if 'e was partial to that kind of stuff. Matchmakers – that it?' She was right, weirdness had intruded. He could not stop. 'Black Magic perhaps? Dairy Box? What about marshmallows?'

'I need a drink. Drink up, Henry. We're going to have a lovely evening.'

'These Turkish Delight are pretty exclusive. You'd remember if your 'usband ever gave a box to Ames-Clegg.'

'Gerry? Give a box to Cyril? Don't be ridiculous. He gave them to me once or twice. Twice at most, he wasn't the greatest spender.'

'Your 'usband?'

'Oh please. Cyril. He's my lover – sorry, was my lover. When he was able to take time off from his horses. Can't we talk about something interesting? Tell me, I've always wanted to know, how much is inspiration, how much perspiration? I mean, does it ever just happen, the whole poem, rhymes and all?'

'Not meaning to pry, Mrs Farnsworth – '

'Olive.'

' – but where was this? Lord North Street?'

'Not actually in the street, Henry.'

'Does your 'usband know?'

'No. This is dreadfully naïve, Henry, but you're the only poet I've met. Now, if you sat down with a title at say nine on a Saturday morning, how long before it was finished? Or does the title come last?'

The foot rocked, the dangling sandal flapped. Peckover tried not to flinch. He judged that if the toe-thong gave way the sandal would strike him in the left eye. His eyes were having difficulty enough in keeping themselves directed at Mrs Farnsworth's eyes and not straying to her armpit. Across her blouse pocket the spangles glinted.

He was uncertain whether he disbelieved her when she said that Ames-Clegg had been her lover or whether he had guessed all along. He pushed the Turkish Delight back into his pocket. Olive Farnsworth was on her feet at the cabinet, then by his chair, topping up his glass. To have moved the glass would be to have had scotch over his fly. They were his last pair of trousers.

'Might I ask how it began, your, ah – affair?'

'Hell, I don't know. How does anything begin?'

'And you'd met 'im before the evening 'e came 'ere?'

'No.'

'So it was through your 'usband – '

'Henry, you've no idea how dull this is. And you a poet. Come on then, I'll show you.'

Bet you will, Peckover thought. But she was gone with her glass out of the door. He hesitated, then stood up with his whisky.

She had paused half way up the stairs, looking round and waiting for him. He followed behind the magenta backside. She walked across a landing and through an open door. Leading up from the landing were more stairs, shabbily carpeted. Through the door the floor covering was linoleum and the room a box-room with trunks, rolls of matting and furniture under dustcovers. 'Wait here, Henry, I'll see if I can find it,' Olive Farnsworth said, putting down her glass on the corner of a teachest and opening a door on the far side of the box-room.

She disappeared through it. Peckover looked out of the window at a grubby sky and dusk settling upon Clapham Common. The half-dozen footballers trotted and kicked. Immediately below in the garden the rose-trees stood to attention. Among the parked cars along the near side of the Common Peckover noticed a maroon Triumph and the trousered legs and lap of someone in the driving seat. A newspaper lay across the lap. Nothing above the lap was visible.

'Here you are, Henry, ninth of October last year. Exhibit number two.'

He turned from the window to receive a ten-inch square photograph; Sir Cyril Ames-Clegg in hunting pink smirking from astride a horse. He or someone had written *Chevalier Silver Cup* and the date across the bottom but no signature or greeting.

'That was the finish, Henry. He had to go into training for the Horse of the Century.' She leaned so close, assisting in observation of the photograph, that her chin was against his shoulder and a mingling of blonde-hair and gin scents infiltrated his nostrils. 'It's a proof copy, he'd never pay money for the real thing. Wait there.'

She vanished again through the inner door. Peckover turned the copy over. *Proof Copy, Hexham & District Evening Mail.* Downstairs a door opened, then closed.

Peckover held his breath and listened. Olive Farnsworth tracked back through the box-room.

'If that's your 'usband – '

'Ssh!' she hissed, flapping her hand. She hurried out to the landing.

'Gerry?' she called down the stairs.

There came a muffled response. What in God's name, wondered Peckover, was he doing in this dreadful box-room, bandaged and hatless, glass in one hand, photograph of a crooked hunting-and-shooting MP in the other, holding his breath and obeying like a child this woman's whim?

'I'm in bed, Gerry! See you in the morning! You all right?'

Again the muffled answer.

'Night, Gerry!'

Smiling at Peckover like a conspirator, she returned to the box-room, closed the door and trod between tea-chests and dustcovers towards the inner room.

'I must say good night, Mrs Farnsworth, and thank – '

'Yes, all right. Hold on a moment.'

She disappeared once more into the inner room. Peck-over listened for the creak of Chief Superintendent Farnsworth's footsteps on the stairs.

He swallowed a long mouthful of scotch and exhaled windily. The stairs failed to creak. If holding on a moment meant giving the Metropolitan police's race relations co-ordinator time to reach the kitchen and start brewing his Horlicks, he would hold on a moment. He turned back to the window. Where, he wanted to know, had he put his hat? In the Triumph the lap was spread with newspaper as though for a picnic. Peckover bent low but even from the base of the window the view permitted nothing above the man's waist. Thirty yards further on, by the telephone-box, his own car was crookedly parked.

'Henry – here a minute!'

Was the summons a semitone lower than the earlier orders? To satisfy a premonition as clear as the photograph in his hand and because he had no aversion to seeing Mrs Farnsworth nude, Peckover obeyed and walked into the inner room, which was the bedroom he had expected, although from where he paused, a pace inside the door, he could see only the foot of the double bed and Mrs Farnsworth not at all. He was troubled by the knowledge that while he was prepared to look he did not want to touch; which was to say that he wanted very much to touch but hoped he would not, life at present being menacing enough without a chief superintendent's wife being added to the assault. Clutching photograph and glass as defensive props, he took another step. The framed print on the further wall was an abstract of intersecting circles. Olive Farnsworth was only half naked, being still magenta trousered, but the sandals had gone and the sleeveless blouse and whatever might have been beneath the blouse. She was not spread out like a houri but seated on the edge of the bed with her forearms crossed across her breasts.

'Hurry up, shut the door. He'll not come up, he never does.'

'I don't pretend to know – '

'We've not slept together for eight years.'

'Your personal – '

'D'you want to draw the curtains? I'm half and half because I'm only half confident. That's a hell of an admission.' She glanced about her on the bed as though for gin but failed to see any. 'You're fairly weird, Henry. It must be the poetry. Come over here.'

Peckover advanced one pace. Smiling up at him, Olive Farnsworth lowered her arms and placed her hands beside her on the bed. She still looked awkward, the seduction seeming to cost her more effort than pleasure.

'If you 'ave more evidence, Mrs Farnsworth,' Peckover started to say, and dried. Evidence of what? His voice sounded episcopal as though forced through a tube. 'Like more evidence,' said a strained voice which he recognized as his own.

'I've this much more,' she said, standing and starting

to laugh. Her fingers at her hip undid buttons.

'No, Mrs Farnsworth.'

'Henry, you're sweet.' A blur of magenta moved downwards. 'Heaven's sake, get rid of that glass and stuff.'

'Mrs Farnsworth – '

'Olive.'

'Olive – '

'Do close the door, Henry.'

Plain white pants, possibly Marks and Sparks like Miriam's, unadorned by lace or hearts or slogans, followed the magenta to the carpet. Peckover, head turned away, opened his mouth but heard nothing. Through the window he saw rooftops and a slate sky. He heard the door close. Then the gin and hair scents were up his nose and fingers were plucking at his collar and tie.

'Unravel your bandage, Henry.'

A fingernail began an advance along his neck. The front of his body had become blanketed in warmth.

'Henry.'

'Olive.'

'Poet.'

In the forward pelvic area or thereabouts considerable heat and tumult was now being generated.

'Oh Henry, sweet.'

'It won't do.' His left hand dropped the photograph and grabbed her wrist. 'It just won't do, Mrs Farnsworth.'

He trod on the photograph. Opening the door he said, 'Sorry. Good night.'

Midway between the dustcovers he heard her voice from the bedroom. 'Sorry! Good night! Copper!' The valediction held more contempt than the blaspheming of a troop of fish porters. 'Right, if you don't want to hear about Beeston!'

Peckover halted. His hand was wet from slopped whisky. He swallowed the last inch and put down the glass on a cardboard carton.

'What about Beeston?' he called.

'What about Beeston?' she mimicked, striding into the box-room. She had put on a bathrobe and was knotting the belt. She did not look at him as she walked past. 'What about Rupert Mountain? What about Gerald Farnsworth?'

He followed her on to the landing and glanced up the stairs and over the banister. The sight of Farnsworth in uniform, holding his cane and regarding him from behind rimless spectacles would have been unwelcome. Farnsworth was not to be seen. From below sounded a grinding, a whirring, then the chiming of the grandfather clock.

'What about Beeston and Rupert Mountain – ?'

'Too late, Henry darling.'

She did not look back. He pursued her down the stairs.

'Mrs Farnsworth, in my capacity as a police – '

'In your capacity as a zero. You want evidence, I'll show you evidence.' She crossed the hall and started down the basement steps. 'Exhibit number three – we up to three now?'

Peckover followed, swaying with whisky, steadying himself with a hand on each wall.

'Mrs Farnsworth – '

'But you can't take it with you,' Olive Farnsworth said, throwing open the study door.

She pulled Peckover by the arm. Though he resisted, holding his ground, he could not help but see into the illuminated waste space of Chief Superintendent Farnsworth's study. The curtains were drawn. A heady smell like the cosmetic department of a Knightsbridge store filtered out into the passage. The desk had been converted into a dressing-table by means of a propped mirror ringed by tubes and bottles. In front of the mirror, his hairy body clad in knickers, brassiere and an auburn wig, sat Farnsworth. He held a lipstick between his fingers and was in profile, except for his head. The rouged and powdered face was turned to the door in horror. The rim-less spectacles had been removed and the eyes ringed with eye-shadow stared at Peckover. The mouth, incompletely red, hung open.

Peckover ran up the stairs and through the hall. He opened the door, stepped into the evening and banged the door shut behind him. Raindrops splashed on his face.

Beyond the parked cars and empty pavements the Common was deserted. He walked past the rose-trees. All that could be seen of the man in the maroon Triumph were fingers holding the newspaper high. Peckover waited on the kerb while a Mini drove past, sidelights twinkling in the gloom. The air was clammy, the rain falling in faster, fatter drops.

He passed behind the Triumph on to the pavement and jerked open the driver's door. The newspaper crackled as the man in the car thrust it aside and gripped the door by the window-frame, trying to pull it shut. He seemed in two minds, one hand tugging at the door, the other reaching towards the glove compartment in front of the passenger seat. His freckled face peered up.

'What 'appened to the Jag, then?' Peckover said, grabbing with both hands the hand and wrist on the window-frame and twisting.

Willie McLeod gasped. His knees went to the floor, his head against the steering-wheel. Peckover twisted and bent until he heard the crack and Willie McLeod screamed.

Through accelerating rain he half walked, half ran to his own car. A solitary figure on the Common was running also, accompanied by a bounding dog.

Peckover swung the car into Clapham Road and cruised north. Man or beast? he wanted to know. Best all round if he locked himself in his seat-belt and drove into the river. Sweat poured down his face. When he tried to look at his wristwatch his hand and arm were so shaking that he had to lay them on the steering-wheel to steady them.

Eight forty-five. More than an hour before the next call to Adamson. Time to look in at his own local and drain his mind.

He had forgotten his hat. The windshield wipers swished, carving twin arcs out of the downpour.

CHAPTER X

'They're so gloomy,' Miriam said.

'I'm not gloomy,' said Peckover. 'I ought to be, considering. But I wouldn't say I was. On the contrary.'

'No one's saying you're gloomy. *They're* gloomy. Fourteen in five days, it's like a factory, and not an ounce of cheer in any of them. Listen to this.'

'You going to read it?'

'Just listen.'

'Quiet, please.' He settled his stockinged feet on the pouf, laced his fingers behind his head and closed his eyes. ''Ouse lights. Orchestra. Curtain.'

Rain gunned the leaded windows. For five days on and off rain had fallen. The cottage carefully had no television but on the radio someone had said that although technically the drought was over, twelve inches of rain would be needed to restore supplies to a meaningful level and render the reservoir situation viable. Peckover felt oddly light-headed. In mackintoshes and gumboots he and Miriam had walked many miles of country lanes, observing the flowers and birds without identifying them. They had hired bicycles and bicycled as far as Cirencester, Chippenham and Avebury. Lunch and supper were salads, an omlette, a pork chop. Not for weeks – years in the opinion of Miriam – had Peckover drunk so little: at noon a pint of ale if they happened to be passing a pub, a glass of wine with supper. By nine-thirty they would be in bed, Miriam with maps and histories, Peckover with *The Old Curiosity Shop*, pressed on him by Miriam. He would fall asleep over *The Old Curiosity Shop* within minutes. After five nights he had reached page eleven.

The rain drummed. Miriam, cushioned and supine along the length of the sofa, read aloud:

> 'If all the dead of all the wars
> Were placed in pairs upon their backs
> With full equipment, ration packs,
> Crossbows and armalites, no pause,
> But stretched twice round this stage, the earth,
> Might God enrage? Might it come home
> Sufficiently to make Him foam?
> Or would he flop about in mirth,
> Share the applause and stand to cries
> Of "Author! Author!" from the pit,
> Swoon at the hilarity of it,
> This cast of dead with marble eyes?
> Who cannot envy them? Far better sense
> To be on stage than in this audience.'

She fell silent, eyeing the manuscript.

Peckover said, 'That all?'

'It's all I've got here. Were there some jokes to go with it?'

'I could write in jokes, don't think I couldn't.'

'I've heard your jokes. It's no wonder there are wars.'

'I don't 'ave to defend it, poetry is its own justification,' Peckover pontificated. Hands behind his head he observed the timbered ceiling. ''Ow about the *Sunday Times*? Might be just what they're after.'

'I'd say the only hope is *Peace News*. But they'll want you to take out a subscription.'

'Can't you use your influence to get a few into the

Quarterly Review of the Royal Archaeological Society?'

'You've no footnotes and they like illustrations – pots and coins.'

'One day I'm going to break into the American market. You wait. They'll 'ave me over on the poetry circuit. The Windy City, Washington 'ostesses. Might even bump into Zadiq.'

'You said we weren't talking about any of that.' Miriam stood up. 'You've been very good so far.'

'Where're you off?'

'Ten-thirty, the Malmesbury shampoo and set. I'll come back transformed, I'm afraid.'

'I'll come with you.'

'Don't want you. Why don't you write an amiable one? Not witty, just amiable. About clowns, something like that.'

'What's amiable about clowns? Suicides, most of 'em.'

'A shining start.' She kissed him. 'See you in a couple of hours. You could do the salad.'

Later he heard the Cortina start away. At the head of a fresh sheet of paper he wrote, The Clown. Sinking deeper into the armchair he wrote: Pagliacci, Popov, Barnum and Bailey, Grock, greasepaint rictus. He wrote 'Grock' once more and underneath, Jock, block, sock, knock, crock, dock, shock, lock. He wondered if the poem were already finished.

His thoughts failed to stay with clowns. Apart from two phone calls from the DC, checking up, the cottage had been a clean break, for Miriam especially. No, that was patronizing, Peckover confessed to himself. For himself especially it had been a break. Stitches and bandages had gone and with them, here in this bosky vacuum, the dross and excess and circling names which for six weeks had hummed in his skull beneath the bandage. Farnsworth, Ann Evans, Zadiq, Beeston, Thomas Mountain, Rupert Mountain, Ames-Clegg. The names had not totally gone, from time to time one would sidle in, but with diminishing frequency. Two days left to go with the birds and flowers; he'd not have said no to another two weeks.

Two days left until what? To what would he be returning in the Smoke? Molehill? Or a counter job in stores and equipment where the ageing and the head cases were sent? The DC's phone calls had offered no hint. Perhaps he had not decided. Or perhaps he'd had private reasons for removing an unreliable inspector from Molehill and was himself now suspect. Someone with a deep pocket had covered up for someone. Like the DC had covered up for Farnsworth.

The clown paper slid to the floor. Peckover dozed. He half opened his eyes to the sound of car gears in the lane. The rain had ceased pattering. According to the clock over the fireplace Miriam had been gone only fifteen minutes. He reached down for the fallen paper. There sounded a knock on the door.

In stockinged feet Peckover crossing the sitting-room, ducked past the open stairway and paused at the dining-room window. The porch could not be seen or whoever was waiting there, but in the lane beyond the gate, between the untrimmed branches of the hawthorn hedge, stretched patches of cream and chrome. Above the hedge, visible from the shoulders up, was a character in a matching cream cap. Unless the hedge had shrunk or the man had climbed on to a crate he must have been formidably large. Peckover trod past bicycles and opened the door. In the porch waited a brown man in smoked glasses and a white suit.

He said, 'Detective-Inspector Peckover?'

'Right,' Peckover said.

'Forgive me, I am – '

'I know who you are. Come in and 'urry up. I'm not 'aving you 'ere when my wife gets back.'

'Your, ah, wife is at Chez Marcel in Malmesbury and I

expect will not be back for some little while.'

Light on his Gucci-shod feet, smiling as if in expectation of great happiness, the visitor stepped inside. His
black sideburns were flecked with white and his smile was
as white as his Yves St Laurent suit. The chain round his
neck was gold, the rings on his fingers were silver and
sapphire and the handbag hanging by a strap from his
fingers was a black cube of doeskin with zip and buckle.
He sauntered forward, glancing in at the kitchen, up the
open stairs and looking about him at timbers, quarry
tiles, rush mats, pine furniture, bicycles.

'Quaint,' he said.

'It's not for sale,' Peckover said, closing the door.

'You are mistaken. Everything is for sale.'

'Cock.'

'Everything and everyone.' The brown man in the
white suit stooped and sniffed a potted dahlia. 'As it
happens, I am not looking for a cottage in this particular
part of nowhere.'

'If you change your mind get in touch with the deputy
commander. If you're not in touch with 'im already.'

'To which bait I shall not rise,' Zadiq said, beaming
and walking on.

'Do we 'ave to sit down,' said Peckover, padding after,
'or can you get to the point without playing around?'

'I have made my point, as I suspect you know. To
everyone his price tag. You are the one playing around.'
Zadiq skirted a trestle-table on which lay Miriam's
sewing. 'You have been trying to find me since that poor
girl was killed. Six weeks, is it? If I walked out now,
offended by your boorishness, I suspect you might try to
stop me.'

'If I tried to stop you, I would. Don't have any doubts.'

'You stop me, my chauffeur stops you. All quite futile.'
They had reached the sitting-room. Zadiq pointed to the
french windows. 'May we go outside?'

'Frightened it's bugged in 'ere?'

'You have the mind of a comic strip.'

'I don't 'ave a gorilla to 'old my 'and and a bag of banknotes for whoever gets in the way.'

'A second-rate comic strip,' Zadiq said, pushing open the french windows. 'Disappointing. I had been informed you were a poet.'

Peckover, tempted, glanced towards the hearth where leaned brass tongs, shovel, poker and toasting fork.

'I would imagine a very minor poet,' Zadiq murmured, walking into the garden.

Beyond the flagged patio the half-acre of back garden was lawn, vegetable patch and a distant wilderness of brambles. The grass was sodden underfoot. Zadiq tested it with his shoe. He stepped back on to the patio.

'Fresher out here. I am passionate about your English countryside.'

When Peckover said nothing but put his hands in his pockets, Zadiq went on, 'You have proved too great an irritation and I want no more of it. No more snooping, no more entering into houses which are no concern of yours, no more breaking of wrists. From now on you will go through the motions and accomplish nothing.' He un-buckled and unzipped the handbag. 'And you will see that your Sergeant Sutton does the same.'

'I see. 'Ow much?'

'Ten,' Zadiq said, holding out a white legal-looking envelope fifteen inches long. 'You have received already five hundred – '

'Which I no longer 'ave because it's in your file – '

'I am aware of that. I said to every man his price and I apologize for the insult. Had I been in London I would not have permitted it.'

' – because it's in your file, I'm telling you, and will be brought in evidence at your trial.'

'The only trial there could possibly be is your own, you

must know that.' Zadiq waggled the envelope. 'You must
also be aware you are an extremely fortunate policeman.
Here, count it.'

'Piss off.'

Zadiq's smile became beatific. 'A hard man,' he said,
and for some moments the pair eyed each other. Between
them on the flagstones detonated raindrops.

Dipping beringed fingers into the handbag, Zadiq
sifted among what Peckover supposed to be sand and
loose lumps of gold. He drew out a roll of banknotes
bound with an elastic band.

'The well is now run dry so far as you are concerned,
Peckover.' He placed the wad inside the envelope.
'Twelve thousand. The well is indeed bottomless but not
for you. You are a pain and I am not risking the added
pain of a suddenly rich policeman. I would prefer a
missing policeman. Here.'

Peckover took the envelope and stuffed it in his hip
pocket. He said, 'A missing policeman? That the way you
manage things in the desert?'

'I know little about the desert.' He was zipping and
buckling his handbag. 'I know that in this country I get
my way.'

'With the assistance of the bottomless well and bruisers
like Willie McLeod.'

'Willie McLeod? Please, I am not an amateur, I do not
hire amateurs.' The smile flashed. 'I might hire you,
possibly, but I do not believe it will be necessary.'

'You git. You creeping bastard.'

'Thank you. I am also very serious. I am not a charity
and I shall not be blackmailed. If you have such ideas
please read your newspapers tomorrow. Perhaps the day
after. You may come across a name familiar to you.'

'What're you talking about?'

'Goodbye, Peckover.'

Business completed, handbag dangling by its strap

from his wrist, Zadiq stepped past Peckover. The policeman grabbed him by the arm.

"Ow long did Farnsworth think about it before 'e went
on your payroll?'

'Farnsworth is not on my payroll. Let me go, please.'

'Beeston's payroll, then. The Mountains'. It all starts
with you.'

'Our agreement, I believe, was no more snooping. I
suggest you begin now.'

'I suggest you learn some elementary facts of life, mate.'

'You are hurting me.'

'I've not even started. I'm going to break your arm.'

'You are the expert.'

'Right. Three places. 'Ere at the wrist, the elbow and
the shoulder. The shoulder's dodgy but it can be done.
What d'you say to that?'

'Let me go.'

'I said what d'you say to that – your arm bust and your
pearly teeth down your throat?'

'If it is Allah's will.'

'Allah's will? It is, that's exactly what it is, Allah's will.'
Peckover, gripping Zadiq's white-sleeved arm at the
wrist and elbow, was breathing hard. 'Where's the grin
gone?'

'Why must you brawl?'

'Who's brawling?'

'You will lose. You will be cut in two.'

Peckover turned his head, following Zadiq's gaze, and
saw the chauffeur watching from the wet grass at the
corner of the cottage. If Willie McLeod was an overweight light-heavyweight, this character was a sumo-
wrestler, hewn from a cliff-face, fed on Arabian rock and
sand. He stood with his legs apart and his hands in his
jacket pockets. The uniform was a tan colour, the peak of
his cream cap veiled his eyes. At least he did not smile.

'That Allah, then?' Peckover breathed, tightening his

grip. Over Zadiq's shoulder he kept his eyes on Cliff-Face
Man, a dozen paces away. His hands began to twist,
creasing the white suit. The sky was sombre and rain
splashed again in fat drops.

Zadiq winced and said, 'Keep on, you will find out who
he is.'

'What's 'is name?'

'Jack.'

'Jack? I like that. Jack the Ripper.'

In Jack's hand had appeared a switchblade knife.
Predictable as Christmas, the bodyguard's greeting card,
Peckover thought. He had faced knives: in Gerrard Street,
at London Bridge Underground, at a café in Ladbroke
Grove, in the Fulham Road after a Chelsea-Liverpool
match. And chairlegs, potatoes with an implanted razor
blade, stone-filled socks. He liked them no better now than
he had in nimbler days, supported by other police. Jack's
knife had clicked open. He held it pointing down, the
blade along the seam of his tan trousers. He started forward.

Peckover released Zadiq, swung about and walked
through the open french windows. He picked up the poker
from the hearth and continued on, through the dining-
room and up the stairs. On the landing he looked back
down the stairs, listening, hearing only rain rattling on
the windows. From the guest bedroom he watched through
the window.

Over the hedge Jack was assisting Zadiq into the back
of the car. The rain beat on his flat cap and on the roof
of the car. He had to crouch low and tuck in his head to
manœuvre his bulk through the door into the driver's
seat. Noiseless in the rain, the cream Cadillac slid along
the lane and out of sight beyond the elms.

Peckover remained at the window watching the August
rain and waiting for his hands to cease shaking. 'Up your
English country garden-O,' he heard himself singing in a

whisper. He transferred the £12,000 from his hip pocket to his jacket hanging in the wardrobe, then ran the bath.

Downstairs in a kitchen cupboard he found cooking sherry, poured three inches into a cup and swallowed it in a gulp. He closed the french windows.

In the bath, soaking and soaping, he estimated there had been between twenty and thirty questions he had wanted to put to Zadiq. The twenty to thirty answers, had he had them, might have gone a fair distance towards putting away the Molehill villains, Zadiq included, until the end of the century. Instead the encounter had revealed three earth-trembling facts.

One, Zadiq was in town. Two, Zadiq had money. Three, Zadiq had support from a half ton of Arabian Gulf rockface named Jack.

Your honour, I rest my case.

Peckover turned on the hot tap with his toe. What was it going to be like to be a missing policeman if missing he became? How expert was Big Jack? No question they were going to have to try because there was no question he could go through the motions accomplishing nothing. If they'd not already guessed that was how it would be they'd know soon enough. Once he might have merely gone through the motions, indeed had done so, five, six weeks ago, from lack of interest. Now it had become personal. Odd how often it happened. You were an impersonal policeman impersonally upholding the law, next you knew you were clobbered on the head, a switchblade was pulled on you, and it was impersonal no longer. What would he do if he were taken off Molehill? Become a lone vigilante?

Peckover dried himself, brushed away the cooking sherry with toothpaste and put on London bobby's holiday rig: chain store trousers, short-sleeved shirt, sandals. In the sitting-room he telephoned the Yard.

Harris, munching, said, 'He was here a moment ago.

I'll ask him to ring you back.'

'You'll look for 'im. I'll 'old on.'

Rain hammered the leaded windows in atonement for drought.

'Sir? Sutton here. How's rural England?'

'Listen, the backhanders are piling up, it's getting like stage money. I've 'ad a visit from Zadiq. Check 'is Regent Tower 'otel. If 'e's not staying there find out where 'e is staying. Don't get close, no free-lancing, 'e's got a nasty-looking chauffeur on a lead. I just don't want to lose 'im.'

'Will do. I collected the second instalment from Mountain's place and that wasn't stage money. Had a haircut and wore my Sunday suit in case I was on camera.'

'Where's the money?'

'Handed it to Inspector Veal, sir. Did you know there was a form for handing on of backhanders?'

'What form?'

'Think it was a T88, sir. No one knows about it except Veal but I had to sign and he signed and we filled in the figure, denominations, time, place, all that.'

'Veal's got forms for 'anging up 'is 'at. What else?'

'Not too much, sir. Your Miss Rifty's back – '

'Save it. Two things. First, the Molehill part five which was lost and is found. See if it 'as a list of shareholders in Mountain's. If there's no list, get one. Know where to go?'

'No, sir.'

'Well, you bloody should, you've been in fraud as long as I 'ave.' Stock Exchange? Peckover wondered. Lloyds? Harrods? 'Ask 'Arris.'

'Sir.'

'Don't sulk. See if the name Gerald Farnsworth's included. Come to that, any of the Greenmead – '

'Chief Superintendent Farnsworth, sir?'

'All you do is look through the list and phone me back. Two, you'll 'ave to get on to the post office for this.' Peckover twisted his ear clockwise, anti-clockwise, and continued twisting. 'Fact is it's not vital, more personal, but see what you can do. I got my sixteen-stitches' worth on the twenty-eighth. Zadiq was either in New York or Zürich or flying between the two. Find out if there was a call from either place to any of our Greenmead boys on the twenty-eighth. Hello?'

'Sir.'

'Thought you'd 'ung up. Stop sulking, man. Twenty-eighth or a day or two before. They must 'ave it stored in a computer somewhere. I'd like it today so tell 'em it's 'ighest priority, red alert, the Russians are coming.'

'When do we see you, sir?'

'Likely tonight.'

He set the table for lunch, transferring to its centre the flowers from the sitting-room. Not good enough, he decided, and transferred them back. Filching the DC's country cottage umbrella from the hall, he tore round the garden snapping off fresh flowers. He peered into the shed for a vase or pot but saw only paint pots, garden tools and cobwebbed soil-filled trays for seedlings. At the back of a kitchen cupboard he discovered a lidless teapot, set the flowers therein and the new centrepiece on the table.

He was rinsing lettuce at the sink when Miriam arrived back. He feigned rapture over her hair though he never much cared for it in the first hours after the hairdresser.

'How's the clown?' she said.

'Incubation stage,' said Peckover, slicing tomato with the dexterity of a man with frostbite. ''Ere's what we do, love. We 'ave a leisurely ale at that 'ostelry with the silent landlord, then lunch, then it's your choice.'

'Has anyone been here?'

''Ere? No. Why d'you ask?'

They drove through the rain to the Two Pigeons. A pair

of farm workers playing darts were the only other customers. Peckover followed his first pint by a second, then
a third. He matched pints with glances at his watch,
though God knew there'd be nothing from Sutton for a
while yet. If Farnsworth were bent, wallowing in Mountain's shares, banking a monthly cheque from the Mountains or Zadiq or Beeston, what in hell did he do? Plug on
in silence and the hope that evidence would drop from the
sky? Tell the DC?

And if the DC were banking Zadiq cheques?

Intercepting Miriam's look, he admitted to her that
just for the moment a cloud had descended. Time was
fleeting, he foresaw the holiday's end. 'Closing-time in the
gardens of Wiltshire,' he said.

'We've two more days – two and a bit,' Miriam ob-
jected.

He could not find the courage to disagree. When the
moment came and he was able to postpone the news no
longer he would need the rest of the cooking sherry.

They went to bed after lunch. Later from the bathroom
Miriam called, 'What's the poker doing here?'

'The poker?' Peckover called back. 'What's the poker
doing there?' He folded an earlobe in two. 'The ballcock
jammed! Bit of an overflow! It's all right now!'

Miriam's choice was walking the four miles to Brink-
worth and four miles back. Chances were they'd be
walking when Sutton phoned back. Still, if he had anything he'd keep phoning. Peckover strode out like the
favourite for the marathon. Frequently he peeped at his
watch. When for the fourth time Miriam complained of
the pace, he explained he had to get to the lavatory. He
didn't know, it might have been the mayonnaise, possibly
the peaches. The telephone was ringing when they
arrived back at the cottage at a quarter past five.

'It'll be someone for the DC,' Peckover said, slamming
the key into the lock.

'Let it ring,' Miriam said.

'Yes,' Peckover agreed, throwing open the door.

He sprinted for the sitting-room.

CHAPTER XI

Even as he snatched up the telephone the final *brr-brr* was surely dying to silence. He knew he was too late.

'Yes?' he said into the telephone.

'Sir? Sutton. I've been trying – '

'Minute.'

Miriam was watching from the doorway. Peckover rested the telephone against his chest and told her, 'The DC. Wants to know how we're getting on. Any message?'

'Tell him about his ballcock,' she said, and walked from the room.

Peckover watched her go. He put the receiver back to his ear.

'Sir – everything all right?'

'Yes, get on with it.'

'First the post office, they're pretty obstructive about the international phone calls. Say they haven't the staff, should be written authority. But they've come back with a cable from Zürich – June twenty-seven. It's to Cyril Ames-Clegg at the Grange, Hexham.'

'Saying?'

' "REFERENCE PECKING PROBLEM SUGGEST IMMEDIATE HOSPITALIZATION STOP WILL REFUND STOP Z" '

Peckover pursed his lips as though about to whistle a tune. Plain enough, he thought.

So for that little job the chain of command, the pecking order for the pecking problem, had been Zadiq, Ames-Clegg, Willie McLeod. Possibly with Ames-Clegg locating his pugilist through the Mountains or Beeston. Was the refund the five hundred sheets in Ames-Clegg's letter-box or was that for some other service rendered?

'I'm collecting a copy, sir, stamped and official and everything.'

'File it. What about the shareholders in Mountain's?'

'No Gerald Farnsworth, sir.'

'You sure? You've searched? You've seen the list?'

'Got the photocopies in front of me, sir. Nine pages. There's an Olive Farnsworth has five thousand quids' worth.'

'Oh?'

'The Mountains hold fifty-one per cent. Beeston has a thousand, Ames-Clegg two thousand – that's pounds. Zadiq's not listed, likely it's too paltry for him. What d'you think?'

'I'm trying not to. Anyone else?'

'Only other name might be significant, sir, that's Malcolm York. He's in for a thousand. They're all very round numbers, wouldn't you say? Almost like they might be birthday presents?'

Malcolm York. Peckover could not at first put a face to the name. In his mind's eye he saw tropical vegetation and a Trotskyite swot pacing between amplifiers.

'All right, well done. I'll be in touch.'

He had hardly put down the telephone before it was ringing again. He picked it up.

'Inspector Peckover?' enquired a man's voice. Peckover would not have bet on whether the voice was familiar or unfamiliar.

'Who's that?'

'Sergeant Windle, sir. Records. Been trying to get your Sergeant Sutton, but – '

'What is it?'

'Sorry to bother you on leave, sir. There's something just come in might interest you. One of your witnesses in that East Middlesex Council business. Malcolm York.

You can cross him off. He's dead.' There came a scraping
sound from records, then the faintest rustle of paper. 'At
his home, if you want it. Four, Parkway, Kingston-on-
Thames – '

'Wait.'

Peckover had begun the mechanical patting of pockets,
searching for a pencil, though he did not need the
address. He had visited No. 4 Parkway. Back into his
mind's eye swam a swot. Crossed off among the greenery.

Asphyxiated by chlorophyll. Digested by baby alligators.

"Ow?" He could find no pencil.

'Throat cut. Only a couple of hours ago. There was a
phone call, no name given. That's all I have. Surrey
police – '

"Old on.'

Miriam had come in with a tea-tray, lemon tea and
macaroons. She composed herself on the sofa, tray on the
rush mat by her feet.

'Thanks anyway, thanks,' Peckover said into the telephone, and hung up.

Miriam said, 'Do I pack?'

'Please, got to think.' He thought with one hand on the
telephone. 'With you in a minute.'

Miriam reached down and poured tea. With assistance
from the operator Peckover got through to the *Evening
Standard* news room. Ross Carter was not there. At a
quarter to six hardly anyone seemed to be there and
neither cajolery nor bluster would elicit a home number
from the twerp at the other end of the line. In the end
sentiment won. He was a boyhood friend of Ross's dad,
Peckover pleaded, in Sydney, known Ross since he was a
baby, two days passing through London. The twerp con-
sented to telephone Carter's home number. Peckover left
his own.

Collecting tea, he risked a glance at Miriam. She was

knitting, impassive. He knew her impassivity. He sat in the armchair and drank tea in silence.

Read your newspapers tomorrow. Perhaps the day after. You may come across a name familiar to you.

Less than two hours ago, Windle had said. Kingston was no great detour for a Cadillac breezing back from Wiltshire to London. What else was it Zadiq had said? *I am not a charity and I shall not be blackmailed.*

Was that what the ex-planning officer to East Middlesex Council had been up to – blackmailing Zadiq? From prosecution witness to bandwagon in one move. Peckover had no difficulty imagining the swot's bitterness. Little wonder there'd been loot enough for shares in Mountain's Ltd. For a time.

I am also very serious.

'Me too mate,' Peckover said.

'Pardon?' said Miriam.

'What? Nothing.'

Peckover swallowed lemon tea. Zadiq was in town, Zadiq had money, Zadiq had support from Rockface Jack. No doubt Zadiq had manicured his nails in the Cadillac while Rockface Jack had entered 4 Parkway, Kingston-on-Thames.

No doubt either about the most sensible solution for Inspector Peckover, fraud squad. A quick shuffle out of it into stores and equipment.

Because Zadiq knew more of what was going on than anyone, Peckover was certain of it, and Zadiq was worried. He was not a charity either. He did not shell out £12,000 to a fraud inspector who was about to be shuffled into stores and equipment. Therefore as far as Zadiq knew, which with his money could be about as far as the horizon, Henry Peckover, Peckover the pain, who would either go slow and accomplish nothing or go missing, was still officer commanding Molehill.

Did that make the DC one more policeman on the straight and narrow, removing a fraud inspector from the firing-line to Wiltshire out of concern for his health? Or was there someone above the DC who had moved in and begun making decisions?

Peckover felt in no rush to return to Molehill. Let at least the blood dry, he considered, on Big Jack's switch-blade.

He was out of his chair at the first ring from the tele-phone. It was Ross Carter.

Peckover said, 'Name you might remember from your Greenmead days, Malcolm York, 'e's just 'ad 'is throat cut. Four, Parkway, Kingston-on-Thames. Get down sharpish you should 'ave it to yourself, before the morn-ings.'

'York? When, why? Christ! This anything to do with Greenmead?'

'Drop in a reference to Greenmead, you won't be far out. Add that arrests are understood to be imminent. Say that. A police spokesman, okay? You keep my name out of it.'

Should cause some twisted knickers among the Mole-hill boyos, Peckover reflected. Investigating Techniques No. 82: If you can't nail a charge on 'em, scare 'em and stand back.

'Arrests imminent in Greenmead Development circles,' Carter said. 'I'll never get that past – '

'You waste a 'orrible lot of time, sport. *Gardening Monthly*'s going to be there before you. 'Ow's the girl – Dizzy Wood, was it?'

'She's in the kitchen.'

'If you want it exclusive you'd better tell 'er you're slipping out for a bag of peanuts. Four, Parkway – '

'Wait. What about your coshing? I could tie in – '

Peckover lowered a finger, breaking the connection. He dialled the Yard. From behind her knitting Miriam

said, 'Happy holiday. Why didn't we book in at a telephone-box?'

He had intended passing his thoughts about Malcolm
York, Zadiq and the chauffeur to Kenneth Long, but
Long was out. He left a message asking Long to call him.

So much, Peckover thought, collecting a macaroon,
for going through the motions and accomplishing nothing. He was not only resting his neck on Jack's chopping-
board, he was even loosening his collar.

Miriam had put down her knitting. 'Nothing like
imminent arrests to round off a holiday,' she said.

'These macaroons taste like soap,' Peckover said, chew-
ing. He added in haste, 'Good quality soap.'

'You do the suitcase, I'll start on the kitchen.'

'What're you on about? You keep talking and sniping.
It's Friday, we've two more days. Pump up your bicycle
tyres. We're doing a brisk twenty miles before supper.'

With the poker in the bicycle basket, he thought. To be
on the safe side.

In Oxford Street, Bond Street and Regent Street foreign
tourists smelling of rain and sweat ransacked the stores.
They spilled westwards into Knightsbridge and the
boutiques along the King's Road. They scooped up knit-
wear, trod through spilled denim and cotton and thrust
armfuls of underwear, bootees and banknotes into the
faces of the salesgirls. Many thousands who had wearied
of buying clothing and some hundreds who had merely
lost their way clamoured in and out of the electronic shops
in Tottenham Court Road acquiring radios and hi-fi
equipment. Umbrella shops were voided and throughout
the West End newly-bought umbrellas were being left in
restaurants and hotel foyers. The polyglot chattering
which in June had filled London with a bee-hum of sound
had become a steady roar punctuated from time to time
by the squeak of a salesgirl flattened against a wall or

crushed between her cash register and the mobs of multi-
coloured customers. Those visitors who were aware of the
day, Saturday, and that tomorrow the shops would be
shut, leaving them nothing to do apart from Speakers'
Corner and the Tower of London, bought with accelerating desperation. Here and there on the fringes hovered a
Briton, watching the scene in wonderment.

In the shared taxi lodged in the traffic in the Edgware
Road the tobacco smoke had become too much for
Thomas Mountain. He pushed down the window and
gulped petrol fumes and dust.

Rupert Mountain on the dickey-seat threw his finished
cigarette out of the window and lit a fresh one. Beeston
blew cigar smoke and coughed. He was not a cigar man,
not like some, Cyril Ames-Clegg and his nine-inch
Havanas for instance. But summoned to The Presence he
needed a prop to promote nonchalance. For the same
reason he had brought Corporal. The golden retriever
sat at his feet, tongue lolling, chops dripping, whisking his
tail.

'Think Cyril'll be there?' Beeston said.

Rupert Mountain shrugged. The father, inhaling a
mixture of ripe tobacco and petrol fumes, was silent. The
cab negotiated Marble Arch and headed along Park Lane.
Only once before had they been called to the Regent
Tower like this, at no notice. That occasion had been
Zadiq's birthday. He had signed for the purchase of the
Regent Tower, the Greenmead Development was at its
palmiest, honeymoon stage, the champagne had popped
and fizzed, freeloaders from the press had attended. A
time of prospects, romance and killings all round.

Cash killings, not people killings. Beeston flicked
cigar ash. All they had received this time was the summons to attend and to look at the front page of the
Evening Standard if they had not already seen it. Now
Thomas Mountain had a copy in his pocket, Rupert a copy

in his briefcase, and Beeston a copy in his lap. The press
were unlikely to be in attendance this morning. Zadiq,
through his smiling, had sounded like someone who had
had his fill of the press.

There were only four paragraphs but they constituted
the second story after headlines on new moves to defend
the pound. Beeston unfolded the newspaper. There was a
byline by Ross Carter, the foot-in-the-door man they'd
had to have removed from the local rag, as they'd had to
have York removed from the council. Intense from the
print stared a photograph of a spectacled man with lank
damp hair.

Malcolm York, the architect who was one of the central
figures in the row over contracts for the controversial
Greenmead Development, has been found dead with
throat wounds at his riverside home in Kingston-on-
Thames. Police are treating the case as murder.

York, 38, first caught the public eye as designer of
Truscott House in Liverpool for which he won the
Arnsen Medal. He accepted the top planning post at
East Middlesex Council because of what he described as
'the exciting challenge' of the Greenmead Development but soon clashed with Alderman Basil Beeston,
leader of the Tory majority, over the distribution of
contracts. He resigned after a vote of no confidence
following allegations that too many contracts were
being awarded to Thomas Mountain and Son, the
Middlesex building contractor.

Sheikh Mohammed Zadiq, developer of the private
estate and link road which is integral to Greenmead,
and a business colleague of Alderman Beeston and Mr
Thomas Mountain, was today unavailable for comment in his eighteenth-floor suite at the Regent Tower
Hotel, Mayfair. Sheikh Zadiq bought the Regent

Tower for his Gulf Consortium at an estimated £9 million.

Scotland Yard's dossier on alleged bribery and corrupt practices in the Greenmead affair has not been closed. A policeman said today that investigations were continuing.

Beeston rolled up the newspaper. He said, 'The bugger threatened me. I paid him three hundred. But I never wanted this.'

'If it's confession time he got five out of me,' Thomas Mountain said.

Beeston leaned across Mountain and threw the cigar out of the window. 'So what's the betting he put the squeeze on Zadiq?'

No one was betting. The taxi drew up at the colonnaded entrance to the Regent Tower and a flunkey in a verdant uniform opened the door. The Greenmead trio had hardly reached the steps up to the glass entrance before reporters swarmed about them.

'No comment, lads, y'know how it is, be fair now, let the dog see the rabbit.' Beeston, breezily jovial, pushed his way forward. He could have put a knee in the crotch of every last one of them. 'Later, lads. We'll all have a drink.'

Corporal tugged on the leash, assisting his master onwards past doormen, through glass doors and into the scented heights of the foyer. The Mountains shouldered behind him, mouths shut. A party of American women with name-tags on their bosoms stood with suitcases and tired faces. Beeston noticed two men in lightweight suits watching him from the magazine bar. The faces were unfamiliar but he smelled police.

At the eighteenth floor they alighted from the lift into the arms of a dapper Arab with pomaded hair. He looked men and dog up and down, seemed to sneer, then pointed them along a plushly carpeted corridor. The scent smell

persisted. Half way along the corridor another Arab
blocked the way. He wore beige slacks, a pink silk shirt and
a silver necklace. He opened a door, allowing dog and
Greenmead threesome into a room like a first-class lounge
on a cruise ship but loud and messy with trays of unfinished food on chairs and a colour television screen
booming out the runners for the first race at Sandown.
On a sofa in front of the screen sat two robed Arabs with
cans of beer in their hands. A third Arab watched the
screen cross-legged on a cushion. A fourth in cotton
trousers and shirt simultaneously watched and talked
into a telephone, placing bets. Their heads turned towards
the visitors but they did not stand up.

Only the fifth occupant of the first-class lounge advanced in greeting, flashing his vote-getter's smile.

Peckover returned early on Monday to the Yard and a
spooky feeling that he had never been away. In Victoria
Street he had kissed Miriam goodbye and she had driven
on to the Royal Archaeological Society with wild flowers
on the back seat and in her ears murmurs of love and
gratitude for the week which had gone, and a warning
that he might be late home. Peckover believed he might
be late home or very early, depending on whether he were
to remain with Molehill or clear out his desk. If the latter
he might, he supposed, be home by noon.

Three new boxes of geraniums had been placed on the
window-ledge outside the visitors' waiting-room. Peckover looked about him and twice glanced over his shoulder
as he strode past glass and concrete to the CID door. To
be mortally cut down now, on the steps of New Scotland
Yard, that would have been a story for Ross Carter to get
his Aussie teeth into. Within three minutes of mounting
the steps and entering the Yard he was fairly certain he
would be home late.

The desk sergeant nodded in his direction, lifted an

automatic hand and resumed his contemplation of space.
In the lift, Lockyer from forensic said, 'Morning, Henry,'
and carried on with the *Telegraph* crossword. In the fraud
office, Sands said with feigned interest, 'Good holiday,
Mr Peckover?' Harris had arranged beside his typewriter
a sunset-coloured fruit or vegetable which Peckover was
no more able to identify than he had the bladderwort and
rosebay willow herb in the rural ditches. Sutton was not in.
Pensionable Milton too was absent; shopping, Peckover
supposed, with his mother.

At his desk he discovered a memorandum from Sutton
listing developments already relayed to him in Wiltshire;
a scribbled note from the same sergeant saying welcome
back, he was off to see Beeston following press reports that
the alderman was about to fly to the Algarve; routine
inter-departmental rubbish; and a meagre sheaf which
included unrevealing reports on two murders – Ann
Evans and Malcolm York.

And a feeling of safety. No longer did he find himself
awaiting the heat of Jack's breath on the back of his neck.

The moment he stepped outside he would be nervous
again of that hot breath because from all the indications
and more particularly from lack of indications to the
contrary he was still Mr Molehill. Why was his telephone
not ringing, bringing the order to clear his desk? Where
were the sealed directives summoning him before the DC?
For country talk if for nothing else?

He flipped through the memoranda and directives,
initialling. He telephoned Veal and said, "Ello? 'Enry
Peckover 'ere.'

'Henry! Just doing my coupon. Coming to see Arsenal
next Saturday?'

The background swishing, was that Veal putting aside
the telephone so that he could rub his hands? Veal was
Arsenal-crazy. His son aged seventeen played for the
reserves.

'How were the green fields?' Veal said. 'Didn't expect you in today. Thought you'd be down at Kingston.'

'Just off. Is Long there?'

'Living there, practically. Probably got his own gas-ring in the incident room.'

'The DC doesn't want to see me?'

'Sick leave. He's been away since Thursday.' Veal received no reply and went on, 'See your bribe money's stacking up, Henry. You must be like a bookie's office in fraud. What've you got up there – the Peckover and District Bribe Bank?'

'I'd sooner win the pools, mate. Spurs five, Arsenal nil.'

'Gaah, what d'you – '

'Tell your boy to get 'imself a transfer to Spurs and stop messing about with the cripples.'

'Gaaaaah!'

For forty minutes Peckover wrote, typed and retyped his report on the visit to the Wiltshire cottage of Zadiq and his chauffeur. He told Sands he was off to Kingston, gathered his hat and left the Yard. At the Kozy Kafeteria in Victoria Street he collected tea and a doughnut and sat at an empty table where he could watch the door.

Ames-Clegg first, if he were at home. Then Kingston. Peckover bit into the doughnut. He was back in the saddle. Any reshuffling, Veal would have known. Except in the case of reshuffled top brass. The DC's sick leave held two possibilities. Either he was sick or he had been quietly suspended from duties pending enquiries under section 49 of the Police Act.

Peckover watched an outsize figure lumber in through the door of the Kozy Kafeteria. Black, boiler-suited, carrying a canvas bag of tools. Not Big Jack. He finished the tea and collected a second cup.

So he was the Peckover and District Bribe Bank, was he? Assets to date, £22,000. The Beeston and Mountains'

£250 plus £250, the Zadiq £12,000 and the Ames-Clegg £500 which was the tricky one, locked in Sutton's desk. The only way he saw of extricating himself from the £500 mess was a clean breast to the DC, or the DC's successor. If he managed to pin corruption charges on Ames-Clegg and bring in evidence the £500 and the unintelligible statement from the Crédit Suisse in Zürich, that just might get him off the hook.

Pin corruption charges on Ames-Clegg? A hunting, shooting, show-jumping Tory MP and crony of peers, prime ministers, bishops and judges? Peckover dodged through the traffic and walked, vigilant, down Great Smith Street. As hopeless trying to crack the Ames-Cleggs of the country as it was a top copper like the DC. Or the Co-ordinator (Metropolitan Area), Community Relations.

He had not a scrap of evidence that Farnsworth was or had ever been pocketing bundles dealt out by the Greenmead crew. Neither was there anything weightier than gut feeling that Farnsworth had nicked then returned part five of Molehill, having first lifted from it the list of Mountain's shareholders and who knew what else? Any gift of £5000 shares given to him he might have asked to be registered in his wife's name as a precaution. A precaution so feeble as to be pointless. More likely the cast-off mistress of Ames-Clegg had herself received the shares as a gift. Ames-Clegg probably had got them cheap. Farnsworth might be bent but he was not stupid, he'd never accept anything so obvious as shares in Mountain's.

Another gut feeling, felt Peckover, turning into Peter Street, was that Farnsworth had engineered his own shuffle out of fraud. Farnsworth might have become scared at the velocity with which the corruption carousel was revolving. Perhaps he was scared of Zadiq. Who wouldn't be? Perhaps he had suffered from conscience and chosen to mend his ways.

As for dressing-up, that was his business.

Peckover lifted and let fall the brass knocker of the house in Lord North Street.

He stood back and observed the house, stepped forward again, tapped his foot. The door opened. A scrawny beauty of yesteryear, pink and angular in tweed skirt, cardigan and single row of pearls, looked him over as she might have looked over a gammon in Harrods food hall.

'Name's 'Arris, Scotland Yard,' Peckover said, raising his hat. 'Lady Ames-Clegg?'

'Hng,' Lady Ames-Clegg said.

'Might Sir Cyril be available for a word?'

'Is it our burglary?'

'Exactly.'

'I suppose you'd better come in.'

He failed to resist a glance at the wire cage of the letter-box as she closed the door behind him.

'You'd better wait in there,' her ladyship said, opening a door to the left of the hall. 'Such an appalling bore all this. Don't touch anything, it's been cleaned.'

He passed through the door. In an earlier age, he believed, she would have called him 'fellow'.

Bookcase, armchairs, photographs, cabinet stocked like a supermarket's liquor shelves. Less one half-size bottle of rum.

'Cyril!' The voice shrilled along the corridor and through the house. 'It's policemen again!'

Roll-top desk filled with papers, gun licences, cricket photographs, riding rosettes, tidy college and regimental scarves, and a blank space where there had been Ali Izmir Turkish Delight. Beside the desk the cube of green steel safe. Ames-Clegg, ruddy and bony, loped in with twine in one hand, secateurs in the other.

'Morning. Sit down if you want. Too much to expect you're going to tell me you've caught the blighters, what?' There was soil on the MP's gardening shoes, a knotted silk square round his neck. 'Keep it short. Have I seen you before?'

'No.' Peckover remained standing. "Ow about Willie McLeod, Sir Cyril? Mind telling me when you last saw 'im?'

'Willie McLeod?'

'We've reason to believe that on June twenty-seven you received a wire from Zürich suggesting you get in touch with Willie McLeod.' Peckover observed a reddening of the MP's complexion. 'Incidentally, it's my duty to advise you – '

'What did you say your name was?'

'It's my duty to advise you – '

'You're not the one who's been prying and nosing and disgracing every tradition of British law enforcement? The one who came to Hexham? Pickwick, is it?' The expression had become incredulous, the complexion crimson. The hands holding twine and secateurs were starting to tremble. 'Picklock – that's more like it! Picklocking and prying while we were in France, because it wouldn't surprise – '

'I 'ave to advise you – '

'D'you have a warrant?' Ames-Clegg shouted.

'I was invited in by your wife. I suggest you calm down and answer the questions.'

'I suggest you get out!' Ames-Clegg stood aside and pointed with shaking secateurs at the door into the hall. 'Don't think this is the end of it! I have friends, Picklock! In the Home Office, the chief constable of Middlesex – '

'Beeston on the police committee. Farnsworth – '

'Out!'

Peckover saw nothing to be won by staying. The man was mad. Keeping his eye on the secateurs, Peckover put on his hat and walked from the room. Lady Ames-Clegg had arrived in the corridor with a milk jug and a look of enquiry.

'Cyril – ?'

'Out!' Sir Cyril Ames-Clegg cried along the corridor.

Peckover did not look round. He opened the front door. There would be other times, other places. Like a bare interviewing room at the Yard. Eventually the Old Bailey. A knee thudded into the small of his back.

The blow sent Peckover careering down the steps. One hand caught hold of the railings and he swung in a semi-circle. He heard the door slam as he reeled diagonally into the railings. His feet skidded through air and he sat with grazed knuckles and bruised arm and shoulder on the pavement.

'God,' Peckover breathed as much in amazement as in pain.

He struggled up, straightening his hat before the house-wife with the poodle on the far pavement could come to him with comfort.

A dozen paces from the woman with the dog a cream Cadillac chauffeured by Big Jack, in the back a dazzle of white suit and teeth, slid away from the kerb, accelerated more or less soundlessly along Lord North Street and turned from sight into Smith Square.

CHAPTER XII

'Deep down they're peasants,' said Olympia Rift. 'Even Zadiq. They might call themselves princes and sultans but they're desert bumpkins really. I mean, they lounge around in their sheets jabbering and drinking with the telly blasting and the girls are just part of the furniture, though they're paying for them. They've not enough to do, that's my opinion, only buying things. Every now and then one of them might take a girl into the bedroom but it's all very quick. They hawk and spit quite a lot. They're not what you'd call *au fait* with drawing-room etiquette.'

Not like you, dear, Peckover thought, watching Rifty raise her bone china cup to her lips, little finger crooked. 'Actually the girls rather like them. I do too, I'd never say no to Zadiq. But I mean they're quite clean and they don't argue, not unless they think you're being grabby, and of course they're oozing money. They keep it in bundles in envelopes. They can be very generous. They've all got wives stashed away in service flats or back in the desert but they never talk about them, they don't go weepy and sentimental on you like some of the Europeans and the Yanks. 'Course, half of them can't speak English anyway. What did you do to your knuckles?'

'I bite them.'

Rifty giggled. Her suggestion had been the tea-room at Fortnum and Mason whither she had arrived to turned heads and whispers; a blonde, ripening woman in aquamarine jeans, polo-neck sweater and Liberty's wool shawl, a little past featuring in Bacardi advertisements but manifestly a consort for reigning Hollywood stags and deposed royalty had she been so inclined. She had requested the Darjeeling and a Danish pastry but after one delicate forkful of the pastry she had pushed the plate aside and lit a cigarette. Drawing-room etiquette, Peckover supposed.

"Ow long did you look after Ann Evans?"

'Personally or on the books?'

'Personally.'

'Seven or eight weeks. She was hardly what you'd call an adventure. Tell the truth she could be pretty objectionable.'

'Then you set 'er up in Rydal Street – gave 'er a start?'

'She couldn't have had a better one. I've got crowned heads on my register.' Rifty paused as though in anticipation of applause. 'Poor girl.'

'You sent 'er Zadiq?'

'Among others.'

'Like who?'

'No one you'd be interested in. Wasn't me sent her the MP, whassisname, and the alderman and that builder, Rupert Mountain, all the business colleagues in that Greenmead nonsense. That was Zadiq. I never set eyes on any of that lot and I never got a penny commission. We'd quite a fight about it.'

'You and Zadiq?'

'Me and Zadiq, me and Ann.'

'Zadiq and Ann?'

'What about them?'

'Did they fight?'

'Why would they?'

'You tell me, you knew 'er. Would you say she'd be adventurous enough to try 'er 'and at blackmailing Zadiq?'

'Never.'

'Someone knocked off 'er 'andbag and everything she might 'ave 'ad in the way of letters, insurance, driving licence – '

'She didn't drive.'

' – as if whoever killed 'er, if they're the same, made a quick collection in the 'ope of netting anything embarrassing. Did Zadiq send 'er Malcolm York?'

'Who's he?'

Who indeed? Peckover wondered. With sundry unfamiliar Surrey detectives and Ken Long at his most obstructive, in the incident room at Kingston and later treading through greenery in Malcolm York's house, he had passed the previous afternoon failing to substantiate his opinion on the why and wherefore of the architect's murder. No hint of blackmailing endeavours among York's papers and bank statements. No evidence of Rockface Jack having trampled through the banana trees. Not that there was likely to have been.

On the other hand, no summons to appear before whoever was filling in for the DC. No complaints from Ames-
Clegg of fraud squad insolence, intimidation and invasion
of privacy. Either Ames-Clegg did not care to risk in-
volving himself with complaints, which was likely, or
someone among the top brass was on Henry Peckover's
side, which seemed increasingly likely. Peckover of fraud
was being given his head.

So the farce continued. Sutton had abandoned credit
cards as though they were drink and he had taken the
pledge; this morning he was trying to locate a partner on
the Gulf Consortium who was rumoured to have fallen
out with Zadiq. Beeston had caught a British Airways
flight to the Algarve. The Co-ordinator (Metropolitan
Area), Community Relations, for all Peckover knew, was
preparing press releases on recent achievements in community relations.

Rifty was saying, 'Wait, Malcolm York – that the one
in Kingston in the papers?'

Peckover waited.

'Never heard of him until a couple of days ago.' She
tapped her cigarette. Missing the ashtray, not for the first
time, the ash dripped on the white linen cloth. 'I'm only
guessing but if you want to know about Ann, and this
York for all I know, you should try closer to home.'

'Go on.'

'I'm mentioning no names.'

'Drink up, Rifty. We're going to take a look at that
clients' register.'

'He's not in it.'

'Who isn't?'

'Please, no names. I've got professional ethics.'

'In fact I'm going to have to borrow it. Extended loan.
Should make racy reading round the Yard. C'mon. You
look after your professional ethics, I'll look after the
register.'

'You're not being fair. The register's my living. I didn't have to talk to you.'

'Don't mess me about. I 'aven't time.'

Over Rifty's shawled shoulders he watched Big Jack seating himself at a table by the steps leading down to the food hall. He was alone and out of uniform, chest and biceps bulging through a grey V-neck jersey. His hair was black curls, his features unexceptional if no exception were taken to features magnified beyond the outsize and arranged on a head with the dimensions of a New Year's Eve balloon. Several morning tea-drinkers had switched their interest from Rifty to Big Jack. He was not reading the menu but regarding Peckover over its top edge.

Peckover met and held the gaze. Was this the psychological softening up? The prelude to the non-psychological switchblade? Any trouble, he'd never make it past Jack down the steps. Behind him was a serving counter and curtains opening probably on to kitchens and exits.

'I assume we're talking about Farnsworth,' he told Rifty.

Though she shrugged her shawled shoulders she seemed relieved. She had named no names, ethics had been preserved. 'He's mixed up in it all, isn't he?'

'In all what?'

'Now who's messing about? Greenmead.' She dripped ash a centimetre wide of the ashtray. 'That's what you're on about, isn't it? Farnsworth used to come calling on Zadiq and the MP and the lot of them before he got shunted to the nig-nogs.'

''E would. It was 'is job. Nothing strange about that.'

'Never said there was, did I? Bit off, though, when the wife comes calling. Not at the same time, I might add. And they go trooping off like a shuttle service down to Clapham Common.'

'Olive Farnsworth?'

'Telling you, wish I had her on the books. I'd make a packet.'

'Who's your source, Rifty? Zadiq?'

'Pity's sake, Mr Peckover, don't let on to him I told you. Biggest pimp in London. Don't know why he bothers with oil.'

'I'd like to get this right.' Peckover watched Jack giving his order to a starched waitress. 'You're saying Zadiq sends 'is Greenmead colleagues off to Olive Farnsworth to partake of 'er favours?'

'Partake of her favours,' Rifty echoed, delighted.

'Is 'e still going to bed with Mrs Farnsworth?'

'Couldn't tell you. Haven't seen him for two months.' Another worm of ash flopped on the tablecloth. 'He wasn't. Not since he met Ann – and probably a couple of dozen others. Mind you, I doubt any of them kept up with the Farnsworth amateur for more than a couple of sessions.' Into 'the Farnsworth amateur' Olympia Rifty injected a knockout dose of contempt. 'What I gather, she set a pretty hot pace.'

'Damn right,' Peckover said.

'What?'

'More tea?'

'No. You still taking my register?'

'No need, thanks.'

'If you want the dirt – I got this from Ann – the MP's horny as hell. Can't get enough of it. The young builder – Rupert Mountain, is it? – he's a spanker. No idea how he made out with the copper's wife but Ann wasn't having any. And the alderman, what's his name?'

'Beeston.'

'All gas and speed. That's what Ann said – "all gas and speed." Isn't that priceless?'

'Why don't you try contact lenses?' Peckover said, reaching out and guiding Rifty's hand before she stubbed out the cigarette on the cloth.

With his other hand he signalled to the waitress. At the table by the steps, beyond the chatter and chinking tea-cups at intervening tables, Big Jack's waitress had set down coffee, ice-cream and a dish of buttered muffins. Enough for a string orchestra, in Peckover's estimation.

'Time to go, Rifty. I'll do the bill. I'll call you some time.'

Rifty swivelled and looked over her shoulder. She reached to the floor and gathered her handbag. 'See what you mean. I'm off then.'

'Know 'im?'

'Happy to say I don't. Looks like publicity for anabolic steroids. Honestly, can't you see why a girl gets turned off?' She kissed her forefinger and touched it to Peckover's forehead. 'With exceptions, Mr Peckover.'

Jaunty, a woman accustomed to being watched, she swung away between tables, past Big Jack, down the carpeted steps and through the food hall. Peckover poured coins on to the bill. Big Jack's munching rate had accelerated. Swallowing coffee, watching Peckover, he pushed his chair back. Peckover poured himself Darjeeling and brought from his pocket the *Express*. He unfolded it at the features page.

Peckover studied the features page. When he glanced up, Big Jack with his elbows on the table was munching muffin and looking towards the food hall. Peckover, hat in his right hand, walked fast between the tables. A stride from the steps he stumbled, bumping against Big Jack's table. His left hand reached out for support and skidded across the table despatching coffee-pot, cup, milk, muffins, ice-cream, sugar, milk and tablecloth into Big Jack's lap.

Peckover took the steps in a single stride. He skirted the cheese counter, side-stepped a morning-suited assistant and edged past startled customers, brushing with elbows and hips the bottled *pruneaux d'Agen*, tinned truffles,

kumquats, honey, hampers. He heard shouts. Already he
was through the doors and into Piccadilly.

Neither running nor looking behind but striding hard,
regarding his watch, a man with an appointment, Peckover swerved into St James's Street. He weaved between
buses, taxis, a Rolls-Royce with a CD plate. A hurrying
man with a hat and an appointment of extreme urgency.

Cleveland Row. Stable Yard Road. The Mall. A man
with an appointment with royalty? Peckover slowed and
looked back. No one showed interest in him. He continued briskly in the direction of Buckingham Palace,
against the tourist tide drifting from the Changing the
Guard.

Clouds like porridge had expunged the sun. Peckover
crossed The Mall. He was confused and frightened, not
least by his own behaviour, and in need of something
stronger than Darjeeling. Fifteen, twenty minutes would
bring him to the Yard. The Horse and Groom would be
hardly even a detour. Thirty minutes, call it, including the
detour.

He looked at his watch. This time the dial registered. A
few minutes before eleven-thirty.

A few minutes after three o'clock, awash but with his
thirst quenched, Detective-Inspector Peckover settled his
hat on his head and walked from the Horse and Groom.

In the course of duty he had cerebrated as to whether
he were investigating local government corruption or
crimes passionelles; or one *crime passionelle*, Ann Evans, and
one crime of blackmail, Malcolm York. He had arrived
at no conclusion. He had written in his mind and rejected
the opening three lines of a poem provisionally titled
'Drowning Not Clowning'. He had discussed the state of
the economy with the landlord, the secret of Gene
Autry's success with a Chelsea Pensioner, and with two
plasterers in dusty dungarees the root causes behind

England's defeat in the fourth Test. Peckover had not been aware that England had been defeated in the fourth Test but he had found himself giving compelling reasons for their failure. To an already obese Dalmatian belonging to a crone in bedroom slippers he had fed a cheese sandwich and a packet of potato crisps.

He walked a straight line along the pavement, exhaling hard from time to time in the belief that this might rid his breath of beer fumes. He approached the Yard from the rear, between concrete heights and behind a plot of grass decorated with a bronze faun-child in flight. Two familiar faces passed him, nodding, to which he tipped his hat in return.

No Big Jack. As he advanced on the CID door, it opened. Chief Superintendent Farnsworth stepped out.

Other than stooping to tie a shoelace or inspect the grass Peckover saw no way of avoiding him. They had not set eyes on one another since an evening at Clapham Avenue South almost a fortnight ago. Soon many questions were going to have to be put to Farnsworth, but almost certainly not by himself and not here on the steps of the Yard. Peckover opened his mouth to murmur a greeting.

Farnsworth walked past without a look or a word.

'The commissioner rang, sir, asked if you were available,' Sergeant Sutton said in a reverential voice.

The team were at their desks in the fraud room: Sands, Milton, Harris, equally impressed by the enquiry from the commissioner. They simulated work while watching the inspector for reactions. Peckover hung up his hat, which fell to the floor. He hung it again with careful nonchalance.

'I'm available,' he said.

'He said it wasn't urgent, he'd ring again some time.'

'Some time?'

'What he said, sir.'

Peckover sat at his bleak desk. He bent out of sight, opened a bottom drawer, saw an unused calculator and meaningless folders, and exhaled into the drawer a fiery gust of beer fumes. He pushed the drawer shut.

'Over 'ere, Sergeant. Bring your chair. Rest of you, if you've nothing else, I can give you thirty or forty jobs on something called Molehill.'

Harris, Milton and Sands became active with papers. When the telephone rang on pensionable Milton's desk he snatched it up, turned his back on the fraud room and whispered into the mouthpiece, 'Mummy?' Detective Sergeant Sutton dragged a chair and sat alongside Peckover, not too close. Peckover tapped the edges of the six Molehill files on the desk in front of him, making them flush.

'Not urgent, eh?'

'No, sir. He sounded fairly affable. Can't think why. We've had one or two developments.'

'Mr Farnsworth?'

'He visited Beeston at his house on the morning Ann Evans was found. That's to say before she was found. He arrived about seven-thirty and stayed fifteen minutes.'

"Ow do we know?'

'Inspector Long, sir. One of his team to be precise – Tommy Roberts. They've been digging.'

"Ow do they know?'

'Milkman, sir, confirmed by a neighbour. They recognized Mr Farnsworth from when he was in fraud and called once or twice in a squad car. Can't confirm it with Beeston because he's off on his holidays again.' Sutton inclined back, out of range of the inspector's breath. 'Mr Farnsworth could've been tidying up a few Molehill ends, I suppose, though hardly a week after he'd been promoted to the community relations thing, and it's odd he never mentioned it to anyone. Still, might mean nothing.'

'Means plenty, lad. Has this visit to Beeston been put to 'im – to Farnsworth?'

'No, sir. Long passed it to the commissioner and us. Might be what the commissioner wants to see you about.'

Peckover caressed an earlobe. 'Nothing new on Ames-Clegg?'

'Nothing. What's old is I've still got that five hundred. I'd be happy to be shut of it.'

'It's doing no 'arm. I need a bit more time. Anything else?'

'Mr Farnsworth, sir, I'm afraid.' The sergeant was apologetic. Across the room Harris's grey-ringed eyes looked up, met Peckover's eyes and looked down again. Sutton said, 'Your Miss Rift phoned from her flat in, er – it's on my desk – '

'Eight, Wellington Place. And she's not my Miss Rift.'

'Sir. Anyway, she phoned half an hour ago, said to tell you Mr Farnsworth had just left. He was wanting to know what you'd been asking her at Fortnum's and what she'd told you. Said she'd told him it was none of his business and showed him the door. She asked me to pass the message on.'

'God, 'e's taking risks.' Peckover began stabbing at the earlobe with a pencil. The Greenmead grapevine functioned swiftly: Big Jack, Zadiq, Zadiq to Farnsworth. 'What else she say?'

'Sent you her love, sir.' Quickly the sergeant went on, 'He sounds desperate, sir.'

'What d'you mean?'

'Well.' Sergeant Sutton ran banana-fingers through his blond hair. He studied his knees, crossed his legs. 'I mean, it's ridiculous but just for argument's sake, if Mr Farnsworth was, well, just imagining he might've known this Dawn de Nuit – '

'You mean supposing 'e killed 'er.'

'No, no – !' But Sutton dried. He recrossed his legs,

examined his rugby hands. 'It'd make sense of a few things.'

'More 'n you know, lad. Get on to Long wherever 'e is. See if 'e can remember exactly what Farnsworth did when 'e came into Ann Evans's flat. Where 'e went, every move. In other words, if Farnsworth was at Beeston's 'ouse at seven-thirty and nicked 'is watch, would 'e 'ave planted it in the flat?' Ten to one he could and did, Peckover believed. To confuse poor buggers like Long and himself and to hit at Beeston. Gas and speed Beeston. No husband, even a dresser-up, would be partial to blokes copulating with his wife – would he? Quite a few Farnsworth wouldn't be partial to if he knew about them. 'Where're you off, lad?'

'Phoning Long, sir.'

'Siddown. What about this Gulf Consortium geezer who's supposed to 'ave fought with Zadiq?'

'Dead end, sir. It was last year. He's been back in Bahrain since December.'

'That it, then?'

'Pal of yours picked up by the heavies, sir. Bow Street tomorrow ten o'clock, if you're interested. He was driving up the Old Kent Road with his arm in plaster.'

'Willie McLeod.'

'Goodbye Willie McLeod for eighteen months is my guess.'

'That indictable then, driving with a broken arm?'

'Stolen car, sir. And it's his wrist, not his arm.' Sutton hesitated. 'Seems he's saying you did it.'

'Did what?'

'Bust his wrist, sir.'

"Is word against mine.' Willie McLeod was minor league, Peckover reflected. No problem there. Not like that Ames-Clegg £500, still undisclosed to the High Command. Had he been drunk? What if he slipped it back through the letter-box? Or sent it to Oxfam? 'Suppose they've not picked up a gorilla called Jack with coffee down 'is jersey?'

'Who?'

'Bloke who killed Malcolm York. Ann Evans too, I wouldn't wonder. Telly sets at close range might be 'is style. Long and the Surrey lot say they've questioned 'im and Zadiq into the ground. Nothing. Sweetness and light, alibis from 'ere to forever and name-dropping like you never 'eard. Like the 'Ome Secretary for one. Just a question whether they can be nailed before Jack comes at me with a fresh coffee-pot.'

'Sorry, sir. I'm not clear what you're talking about.'

Peckover gently belched. 'Never admit to being unclear, Sergeant. Everything comes clear in the end. The flash of light that blinds, the London Phil with extra staff on the cymbals. 'Ere's the picture.' A flurry of rain smote the fraud room windows. Peckover picked a loose strand of skin from his grazed knuckles. 'We don't know exactly 'ow deep Mr Farnsworth's pocket is, or come to that whether 'e's ever taken a back'ander in 'is life, but Mrs Farnsworth is an amateur who'll not say no to Turkish Delight. Zadiq is not only your Crœsus for whom everyone is up for sale, but a pimp who spreads 'appiness by sending 'is Greenmead colleagues off to Mrs Farnsworth and probably recommends to them Ann Evans and a few other pros when 'e's feeling expansive. Rupert Mountain's a spanker, Ames-Clegg can't get enough of it and the old boy, Thomas, 'e might be what's called a loose end, which is to say 'is end's loose, past it, because 'e doesn't come into the bed bit, not as far as I can make out. All clear?'

'Yessir. Waiting for the cymbals to clash, sir. My opinion is it's all a handful and we should have a word with the conductor. I mean the commissioner. Or someone.'

'So we shall, lad. Right away. Try Long first.'

Sutton carried his chair back to his desk and telephoned.

Harris had set a snack beside his typewriter in readiness: a polished Granny Smith and a vacuum flask. Peckover opened the top Molehill folder. He thought: I've no objection to the Police Medal for gallantry in the face of fearful odds but I don't want to have to earn it.

Not posthumously. Police work was a mess. If there existed the cymbals, the shaft of sunlight, the four horsemen riding across the sky, trailing revelations, they had never happened to him. They were not going to happen with Molehill either, that he was certain of. Zadiq and Jack just might get put away for murder. But what was there on Farnsworth?

Farnsworth, Ames-Clegg, Beeston, the Mountains, the enquiries might go on for months, years, and in the end fritter out from lack of interest and manpower problems.

Police work was untidy, inconclusive and dangerous. Peckover emitted a beery sigh, amalgam of unease and dissatisfaction. The next move had to be Ames-Clegg again; or worse – Olive Farnsworth. He for one would not be going near Zadiq and his chauffeur. He'd been given his head by, he supposed, the commissioner, he was not passing it on to Big Jack. He was not going anywhere, questioning anyone, without Terry Sutton.

There came a single tap on the door. Veal looked in. Above the handlebar moustache his expression was the mingled shock and euphoria worn by messengers of catastrophe.

'Farnsworth's dead,' he said. 'They think it's Farnsworth. Jumped in front of a train at Green Park Underground.'

CHAPTER XIII

Olive Farnsworth grimaced at the buzz of the front door-bell; a discreet, compassionate buzz, muffled in sympathy.

They wasted no time. Nine o'clock in the morning and already it was starting again. She had not slept, she had not even made coffee yet. If she arrived at the door with the size eleven shoes she was holding, perhaps his ties draped over her arm, would they take the hint and go away?

The commissioner and assistant commissioner had called. A string of lesser hierarchy with hushed voices had called. Her mother had called many times, wanting to move in and remain, revelling in it. Neighbours had called, apart from those who had kept away. Friends of both herself and Gerry had either called or telephoned and others might have a letter in the post. She had been surprised, thinking about it, how few friends either of them had. From Cyril there had been a telegram and telephone calls offering to return to London. God, he'd probably start talking about divorcing his wife now. It would be talk too. He'd produce a love-nest midway between his pads in Westminster, Merioneth and that benighted Hadrian's Wall.

Not a word from Zadiq.

The bell buzzed a longer buzz. Olive Farnsworth put the shoes on a chair and walked from the room. In the hall the grandfather clock whirred and chimed. She opened the front door and said, 'You.'

'Mrs Farnsworth, morning, 'ope I'm not intruding. I'd like to offer my condolences. I'm sincerely sorry. This is Sergeant Sutton.'

'Hello,' she said. 'Thank you.'

'Might we come in a moment?'

'I'd sooner you didn't. The place is a mess and, well, it's all a bit frantic.'

'Someone with you?'

'No.'

'We'll be very brief.'

'No. Please.'

'Only a moment, Mrs Farnsworth. It's in everyone's interest.'

'Really, if you don't mind, no.'

'I don't want to 'ave to insist.'

For a moment Peckover believed he was going to have to. Her eyes had grown wintry and her hand moved as if about to close the door. She wore a woollen dress with a brooch and no make-up. She stepped aside and Peckover entered, hat in hand. Sergeant Sutton trod behind.

The record-player in the sitting-room was silent. Piled on and around the magazines on the coffee-table were police diaries, the chief superintendent's spectacles' cases and a lidless box containing collar studs and cufflinks. Olive Farnsworth opened the cabinet and poured a gin and tonic. She did not offer her visitors a drink or ask them to sit down.

'As you know, Mrs Farnsworth, since I took over Greenmead from your 'usband we've 'ad two violent deaths which may 'ave some connection with the affair. And now, I'm sorry to say, your 'usband.' Peckover stood in the centre of the carpet rotating his hat between his hands. Sutton, hands behind his back, found a discreet square of carpet by the bookcase. 'Without anticipating the coroner, several witnesses 'ave no doubt at all that 'e jumped. I'd like to ask if you've any thoughts why?'

'No.'

'Would you mind trying?'

Olive Farnsworth sat, sipped and opened a magazine. 'He was depressed.'

'Yes?'

'Depressed and depressing. You're all depressing. What I can't understand is why you don't all jump.'

'Anything in particular 'e might 'ave been depressed about?'

She shrugged and turned a page. 'The community relations thing. Blacks and whites. All that.'

'Y'see, Mrs Farnsworth, we believe 'e was well on top of the community relations job.' Peckover sat unasked in the armchair opposite Mrs Farnsworth. How many years since he had sat here with her armpits pointed at him? 'But it's almost as though 'e couldn't let go of Greenmead. 'E was with Alderman Beeston only an hour or two before the body of Ann Evans was found.'

A page of the magazine rustled as it turned.

'And shortly before 'e went to Green Park Tube 'e was visiting a woman who acts as agent for a number of prostitutes including Ann Evans. When she was alive, that is.'

'Really.'

'Trivial enough incidents until you start to add them up.'

'You know more than I do.'

'Perhaps more than you think I know. But there are gaps. It'd be of assistance, Mrs Farnsworth, if you could explain 'ow you came by five thousand pounds of shares in Thomas Mountain and Son.'

Olive Farnsworth did not answer. By the bookcase Sutton put his hands in his jacket pockets, thumbs out.

'Also,' Peckover said, 'your level of intimacy, shall I say, with Mr Zadiq. You'll be aware that any passing mention 'e might 've made to you about Greenmead could be of 'elp.'

No reply.

'Because we know of your 'aving sexual relations with Sir Cyril Ames-Clegg and certain others who 'ave a stake in the Greenmead Development. Rupert Mountain, of course. Beeston. It's a question of gaps, Mrs Farnsworth. Did you see Ann Evans after Zadiq swapped you for 'er – or was it just the once in Rydal Street?'

Still Olive Farnsworth said nothing. She seemed to have shrunk, motionless in the armchair, eyes on the magazine.

"Ow did you do it, Mrs Farnsworth?"

Nothing.

Peckover watched the immobile woman. He could feel the silence of Sutton somewhere behind him.

'I can't believe it was the telly,' Peckover said. 'Not unless she was already lying on the floor.'

'There was a nailfile.'

'On the dressing-table?'

'One of the long ones, on the bed.' Olive Farnsworth spoke in a voice so small that the policeman sitting opposite leaned forward, trying to catch the words. 'She fell down but she was making noises so I dropped the television on her. I couldn't go close, touch her, not again. It wasn't heavy.'

'I must caution you that Sergeant Sutton may take down anything you say and this may be brought in evidence. We'll lock up 'ere, Mrs Farnsworth, and get along to the Yard.'

'None of it was Gerry's fault,' Olive Farnsworth said in the small voice. 'Wasn't his fault he was what he was. He was the only straight one in the whole disgusting mess.' She sniggered, a catarrhal, animal sound, and the magazine slid from her lap to the carpet. 'Someone say straight? Straight copper but a bent husband – bent as a worm. Lipstick, no kids, it's beyond me, what kind of life is that? Why shouldn't I sleep around? Look at it one way it was all his fault.'

'Look at it one way, Mrs Farnsworth, perhaps 'e's well out of it,' Peckover said. He did not want to hear more but if now she needed to talk he had no choice, not this side of callousness. He glanced behind him. Sutton was writing. 'So 'ow did you meet Zadiq?'

'Zadiq was buying up the Greenmead operators and Gerry was on to him. So he made the personal visit to Clapham with money in his handbag. October the seventh. Gerry was out, which didn't bother Zadiq. Took him fifteen minutes to get me into bed.' Again the snigger, except that now the sound was throaty, between a snigger and a sob. 'I lie. Isn't that what you call a euphemism – bed? It was in that chair – your chair, Inspector.'

Her eyes lifted at last. Peckover refused to react.

'I'm not stupid,' she said in the distant voice. 'He wanted it but what he really wanted was me to influence Gerry, tell him to go slow and get rich.'

'Did you?'

'Told you, Gerry never took a penny, ever. Respectability and rectitude, that was Gerry. Dreams of Buckingham Palace and a knighthood. I didn't even try. Two glorious months, the sheikh and me, before his sheikhship cottoned on. Then he registered the five thousand pounds of shares in my name and good night.'

'The parting gift.'

'Zadiq doesn't give gifts. He wanted to terrify Gerry out of his respectability.' She took a swallow of gin, clutched a fold of her hair between her fingers. 'The object was to get some sort of devious hold over him. The wife with shares in the corrupt builders and dealers the husband was investigating. If that came out Gerry would've been out – on his ear.'

Another swallow. She twisted hair round her fingers. She was weeping and her voice had so diminished as to be almost inaudible. Peckover was aware of Sutton close behind his chair, straining to hear.

She said, 'The parting, anyway. He deigned to see me a couple of times at his Regent Tower. He started sending those revolting men as a consolation prize. I hated them, hated them!'

'Why don't we leave it there, Mrs Farnsworth?'

'I tell you I hated them. What did he think I was?'

'Ames-Clegg too – you hated him?'

'That flatulent weed. He'd be someone to run to, he's got influence, he's not short of a penny, but let him choose between me and a horse . . .' The outcome of such a choice was so obvious that Olive Farnsworth could not bring herself to express it. 'Then the Welsh bitch, flaunting her at me. She was young, I was the hag, the has-been. Zadiq knows how to humiliate all right.'

She was weeping openly now, the back of her hand on her forehead. Peckover drew deep breaths. Could she have loved this toe-rag sheikh out of the desert? he wondered. Love him still?

'So you went along to Rydal Street, just to talk, try to persuade her to stay off the grass,' he said softly. 'But she didn't want to know. There was the nailfile. And afterwards – '

'I don't know, I don't know.'

' – afterwards you took 'er 'andbag and papers in case there was something you could use against Zadiq. Something to bring 'im back to you.'

'I don't know. I junked them somewhere. Over Blackfriars Bridge.'

'And you 'ad to tell someone so you told your 'usband that same night. And 'e went off to Beeston's.'

And nicked the watch and planted it in Ann Evans's flat because the husband of a convicted murderess would be unlikely to be high on the list of invitations to Buckingham Palace.

She was sobbing noisily, shaking and trying to drink gin which splashed against her mouth and dribbled down her chin. Her legs stuck straight out and apart.

'Let's leave it, Mrs Farnsworth. No more.'

'No more!' screamed Olive Farnsworth, and threw the glass.

Had she thrown the glass at the policeman leaning towards her, twisting his hat by the brim, she would have brained him. She threw it high and wide. Gin sprinkled the blond hair of Sergeant Sutton. The glass smashed against the wall. Olive Farnsworth shrank sobbing into a heap. Then she prised herself from the armchair and ran from the room.

Sutton pocketed the notebook and started after her.

'Give 'er a minute, lad.'

Peckover drooped. For a few moments he closed his eyes. There was no elation.

'That's it, then,' he heard Sutton say.

'That's it, lad. That's part of it.'

'Yes.' Sutton sat on the sofa and took out his notebook. 'She still doesn't make it clear why Farnsworth killed himself.'

'Why not? You 'eard 'er.' Packover lay back in the armchair. ''E was depressed.'

He had every reason to be. He must have guessed that word of his visit to Rifty would leak round; that the new fraud team would uncover his wife's holdings in Mountain's if they had not done so already; that the DC would not have been sent on sick leave because he was sick; that Malcolm York's murder meant deeper digging; that the *Evening Standard* reference to 'continuing investigations' was too true. Beeston had cleared out. Press and fraud branch were once again tracking after Zadiq, Ames-Clegg, the Mountain father and son. The fraud inspector who had taken over from him and ought to have been dismissed fifty times over for contraventions of law, protocol and good sense had been kept in the saddle. What price respectability and rectitude for Gerald Farnsworth? What kind of future was left to him? Even his most private tastes had been witnessed by the same fraud inspector. For all Farnsworth knew they might be the current laugh at the Yard.

On top of all that he was a cuckold from Clapham to East Middlesex and back. An unstable, violent and promiscuous wife he was unable to rely on even for a dinner-party for colleagues and acquaintances.

Perhaps she loathed all men, Peckover reflected. Cheated out of children and what the books and courts called a normal married life, why shouldn't she revenge herself by humiliating them in whatever way a woman humiliated a man in bed?

He had been wrong too on the Big Jack–Zadiq–Farnsworth grapevine which had tipped off Farnsworth that the fraud inspector and Ann Evans's madame had consorted over tea at Fortnum's. The grapevine probably had been Big Jack–Zadiq–Olive Farnsworth–Farnsworth. Zadiq needing to know what the hell went on, how close the fraud inspector was getting. Now the DC had gone, what closer contact to police sources had he than Olive Farnsworth? Olive Farnsworth, terrified murderess, would have had her ear to the ground on her own account.

She would tip off her husband anyway. He was shielding her, no one else knew how Ann Evans had died. To function as protector he had had to know what was going on.

What did it matter any more? 'Poor bugger,' Peckover said, gazing at the ceiling. 'A lesson to you, Sergeant. Never let your British respectability win over duty. Farnsworth committed two criminal acts in the pursuit of respectability and sod-all good they did 'im.'

'Sir – '

"E nicked Beeston's watch and unloaded it in Ann Evans's flat, and 'e nicked part five of Molehill and its list of shareholders to try and 'ide 'is wife's name.'

'Sir, sorry, I know it's nutty but we've 'ad one suicide.

I don't know where Mrs Farnsworth is but I can't hear – '

'Christ!'

Peckover was out of his chair and sprinting from the sitting-room. 'Downstairs, Sergeant! Kitchen, bog – there's a basement!'

He hurtled up the stairs. Landing. Box-room. Mrs Farnsworth's bedroom with the framed abstract of intersecting circles. For a moment he stood, listening to the silence of the house.

Back to the landing. Peckover threw open doors. An empty bathroom. An empty bedroom with suits, shirts and shoes laid out on the bed and drawers and cupboards open and half cleared. A dressing-room. An empty guest bedroom.

'Sir!'

'Yes!' Peckover cried, leaning over the landing banister.

'No one here! Back door's open – '

'Minute!'

He hurtled up the second flight of stairs, found bare attic rooms, and raced down again, across the landing and down to the hall.

'Sergeant!'

The front door was open. Gusts of Clapham air from the road and from the back garden whirled through the house. Peckover dashed past the rose-trees. Sergeant Sutton was standing on the pavement looking both ways along the road. Cars passed; two boy scouts on bicycles.

'Does she have transport, sir? She must've gone out the back – '

'All cars call, lad – quick! I'll rouse the commissioner!'

Peckover and Sutton collided chest-to-chest.

'Car radio!' Peckover roared, and ran for the telephone in the house.

'Can we give them a clue where she's heading?' Sutton shouted.

'Told you where, didn't she?' Peckover shouted back. 'Ames-Clegg!'

Ames-Clegg, someone to run to, she had said. Wherever Ames-Clegg might be. Constable Armitage, briefed to keep an eye on the house in Lord North Street, had the previous afternoon reported that Sir Cyril and Lady Millicent, with three suitcases and a dog, had driven off in a northerly direction in their Rolls-Royce Silver Shadow.

Peckover seized the telephone in the sitting-room and dialled. In the pause between reaching the Yard switchboard and being put through to the commissioner's office he snatched from the mantelpiece a framed photograph of Olive Farnsworth, laughingly tousled.

Rail being three times as brisk as the three hundred miles of motorway, and the train being due twenty minutes sooner than the first available flight, Detective-Inspector Peckover and Detective-Sergeant Sutton travelled first-class from King's Cross. They read newspapers, ate four courses in the restaurant coach, dozed, stared through the window and made no attempt at conversation. At two-fifteen the train pulled in at Newcastle. Two police cars, a superintendent, a sergeant and four uniformed constables of the Northumbria County Constabulary awaited them. A grander turnout than Peckover had expected.

'No sign of her so far,' the superintendent said. His name was John Crook: meat and drink to colleagues and convicts alike. He had a weatherbeaten aspect and his windcheater and raffish beret were rain-spattered. 'The station here's taken care of. The airport police are alerted and I've got cars the Hexham side of Corbridge, Riding Mill, Whitley Chapel. If she comes any other road she'll likely get through. I haven't the men.'

'I don't want 'er meeting Ames-Clegg.'

'She might make it to his house but she'll not find

Ames-Clegg there. It's the twelfth. He's up on Cheviot Moor.'

Cheviot Moor? The twelfth? The Twelfth Day of Christmas was all that came to Peckover's mind and for a moment he could not recall even what month it was. The superintendent's accent took some following too. Geordie, was it? Out of London, Peckover felt out of place.

'Twelfth of August, sir,' Sergeant Sutton murmured. 'Grouse-shooting.'

'Yes, yes, I know.'

Superintendent Crook said, 'Don't know what you've got in mind exactly. She'll presumably go to the house. On the other hand, if it's Ames-Clegg she wants and she's phoned and knows where he is, she might go to the shoot.'

'You've got someone at the 'ouse, sir?'

'Outside, at the gate lodge. You don't breeze into that place without a warrant and an army of lawyers.' The superintendent plucked off his beret, smoothed an un-smoothable tangle of hair and replaced the beret. 'Peckover, you succeed in putting Ames-Clegg away, we'll send you a bottle of champagne, compliments of the Northumbria police. Pain in the arse for years.'

''Ow far's this Cheviot Moor, then?'

'Forty miles. Half an hour once we're out of the city.' Crook zipped to the neck the last inch of windcheater. 'Wife of that new co-ordinator for race relations, that right? You southerners. Why'd he do it?'

'Depressed.'

'Not surprised if Ames-Clegg was her boy-friend.'

'You're up with the news, sir.'

'Your Inspector Veal on the blower. You're sure she'll come up this way?'

'No.'

He was guessing. The next hour or two should tell. But he had lost her, it was for himself to find her. The Yard could look after the London end.

Damn and hell, where was the woman? So much for feeling sorry for people, allowing them to dry their tears.

He rode with Crook, Sutton and a fat constable in the leading car. The fat constable behind the wheel reached back, handing Peckover a clutch of maps: large-scale, small-scale, tourist, Ordnance Survey. Rain rattled on the windshield. In ten minutes they were in rolling countryside, the road their own. At no time had the constable at the wheel shown an interest in speed limits. Now he trod the accelerator into the floor.

'The shoot's somewhere here beyond Otterburn,' Crook said, stabbing a finger on the Ordnance Survey map open across Peckover's knees. 'Shouldn't be too hard to find. If she's in her husband's car it's a grey Allegro, according to your Inspector Veal.'

Peckover eyed the map. North-west of Newcastle, Cheviot Moor was fawn-coloured emptiness. Thirty or forty miles south, at the third corner of the triangle, was Hexham and Ames-Clegg's place. On the fawn moors he found a wiggling stream, a prehistoric remnant or two and contours implying that some tracts of moor were higher than others. Beyond Otterburn, towards the Cheviot Hills and the Scottish border, were place-names signifying, Peckover supposed, farms. There was nothing which looked as substantial as a village. Mickle Cragg. Shepple. Cold Fell. Kirtle Fell.

They drove in silence. Not a pub in miles, Peckover assumed. Sergeant Sutton popped chewing-gum into his mouth. The rain eased, then ceased, allowing through the washed windows glimpses of blue sky between the clouds. The convoy of two swept through Otterburn into high country then right-turned up a road which Peckover knew would debouch them sooner or later into swamp. He watched the undulating treeless wilderness.

'Should be getting warm, sir,' the constable said.

In the back seat with Superintendent Crook, Peckover

leaned forward and watched through the windshield, seeing only an unending surface of land which was not fawn but black, dipping and rising, and on the horizon the whalebacks of what he supposed to be the Cheviots. Above the hum of the car engine sounded a distant thudding. Then silence. Then another series of thuds. Peckover chanced a sideways glance at the superintendent.

Crook said, 'Speaking for myself I'm inclined to keep in the car. They have a pretty boozy lunch. They can get a bit erratic in the afternoon.'

The landscape was black tinged with mauve. Peckover identified heather. Heather in his experience was sprigs of dusty flora wrapped in silver paper and pressed on you in the street by gipsies in return for money. He had never seen limitless heather such as this. He heard another series of thuds. In the sky appeared a moving, racing shape like a tattered tablecloth, perforated here and there to allow the sun through. Scraps of tablecloth parted from the main mass, wheeling and tumbling.

'There they go,' Crook said.

The car crested a rise in the road. Ahead was parked a fleet of assorted cars. Apart from the racing tablecloth, now napkin-sized and diminishing towards the humped Cheviots, there was no sign of life.

'Slow,' the superintendent told the driver. 'Keep going.'

Somewhere in the vastness dogs were barking. The police cars drove past the parked vehicles. There were Land-Rovers, Minis, two station wagons, a BMW, a Rover and a Rolls-Royce Silver Shadow but no grey Allegro. Sutton flicked pages in his notebook. He said, 'That's the Rolls, sir – Ames-Clegg's.' The convoy continued.

'They'll have at least one more drive, there's a set of butts half a mile on,' Crook said. 'Don't know whether you want to get down to Hexham or hang on. They'll be half an hour getting themselves together.'

'We'll stay with them,' Peckover said.

He was not wholly clear what the superintendent was talking about. Watching through the windows he saw no life, neither human nor bird. Only black heather to the horizon.

'Up there, turn off,' Crook told the constable.

The convoy swung down a track leading into deeper wilderness, reversed through heather and parked in a shallow rain-filled dip in the track. The sky was shadowy again and rain had started to fall. The fat constable wound down his window and lit a cheroot. The superintendent lit a cigarette.

'Well, it's a day out,' said the superintendent.

They could see the road without being seen, or not without being sought after. Sutton read his notebook, Peckover looked from time to time at the map. Rain tipped down, slowed, then stopped. The constable threw his finished cheroot through the window. A Land-Rover passed, then a second Land-Rover, men and dogs in the back of each. A station wagon, the BMW and a third Land-Rover followed. Sutton pocketed his notebook. Peckover folded the map.

Along the road drove the Minis, the Rover, the Rolls with Ames-Clegg in a deerstalker in the front passenger seat, the second station wagon. Peckover watched for a grey Allegro but there was none. The constable switched on the engine.

'Give them a moment,' Crook said.

To the left sounded an explosive banging of wings as a red grouse lifted from the heather and flapped into the sky. The police cars moved back along the track, on to the road and onwards in the wake of the vanished army.

In five minutes they sighted the cars. 'Hold it,' Crook said. The police convoy braked and halted.

The cars ahead had again parked by the roadside. The

Land-Rovers had disappeared. To the north of the road
and moving away from it were a score of figures, strung
out in the black landscape.

'What now?' Crook asked Peckover.

Peckover had wanted to ask the same question. Olive
Farnsworth might have arrived by now at the MP's
mansion at Hexham – and be fleeing from it to God knew
where, warned off by the police presence. She might be
being scraped off the rails of a London Underground. She
did not seem to be here. Was his whole professional life to
be a series of wrong guesses?

'I suppose we've no binoculars?'

The constable at the wheel burrowed in the glove compartment. He reached back with a superior smile and
binoculars. Peckover took them and climbed from the
car.

Thumb and fingers twisted the focus wheel, bringing
into relief a pair of marching figures, one with a gun
under his arm – or two guns, was it? Peckover shifted the
binoculars across the landscape, picking up more striding
men. There were dogs at their heels. A dog and a man
carrying shotguns accompanied Sir Cyril Ames-Clegg in
deerstalker, tweeds and gumboots.

No Mrs Farnsworth. No women at all so far as Peckover
could see.

At his side the superintendent said, 'They're heading
for the butts – see them? Those little turrets.' He sniffed
the air. 'Shouldn't be long. The Land-Rovers are further
on. Not far. The beaters'll probably come that way.' He
pointed across the road towards undulating emptiness to
the south-west. 'They drive them down wind. They'll be
pretty speedy when they come. Sixty miles an hour.'

The birds, Peckover wondered, or the beaters? He
returned to the car and sat watching the tweeded figures
and their dogs vanish one by one, some beyond the
ridges of heather, others blurring into the butts which

dotted the moor at eighty-yard intervals. He tweaked his earlobe in bafflement and frustration, increasingly certain that he ought to have been somewhere else.

But where?

'I'm going to 'ave a word with Ames-Clegg,' he said and climbed once more from the car. ''E wouldn't see me at 'is 'Exham place. Threw me out of 'is 'ouse in London. Third time lucky.'

Crook hesitated then said, 'I'll come with you.'

'With respect, sir, I'd sooner you kept an eye out for that grey Allegro. Don't worry, if there's any boozy shooting starts I'll lie flat on my face.' He handed Crook the photograph filched from the sitting-room in Clapham Avenue South. 'That's 'er, except she probably won't be laughing. If she shows up 'old 'er tight, in a manner of speaking.'

'Ames-Clegg's not going to thank you for invading his butt – in a manner of speaking. There's a fair amount of protocol in this grouse-shoot business.'

'I'm in a fair mood for wrapping 'is protocol round 'is neck.' Peckover stooped and said through the window, 'On your feet, lad. Wind up your calculator. The fraud squad's off to the butts.'

CHAPTER XIV

Peckover felt unaccountably light-headed. The moorland air? Action after so much sitting and waiting? At his first step off the road and into the heather his foot sank ankle-deep in water. He strode on and his other foot submerged in water. The trick, he realized, would have been to keep atop the clumps of heather. Or gumboots.

'Which butt did 'e go to, lad? That one?'

'Didn't see, sir.'

'You try the next along. Any trouble – arrest 'im.'

The closest of the peat turrets was a hundred yards distant. Sutton struck off at a tangent. Peckover rammed his hat lower on his head and paddled through a tract of landscape more like low tide at Weston-super-Mare than Northumbrian moorland. From a butt a voice faintly and indistinctly roared, 'Gerroffa bloody aaagh rnng y' doing!'

Peckover might have roared back but for the explosion of a gun from another butt. Looking up, he saw a half-dozen grouse streaming across the sky. There boomed out two, three explosions. In the sky behind the vanguard of these grouse came more, and behind these still more. They flew in slow motion, it seemed to Peckover, red-black silhouettes vigorously flapping. Far off, beyond the road, he could see the line of beaters like matchstick infantry. He opened his mouth to call to Sutton but the second wave of grouse was overhead, guns boomed, and the sky was filled with flapping tumult.

Peckover dropped into a crouch, balancing himself on a hand which sank into water and peat. In speeded-up action the grouse swept across the clouds. The shotguns banged, black bundles tipped from the sky. Peckover looked for Sutton but failed to see him. Dogs were barking. The guns banged without pause as the grouse soared over the butts.

Peckover rose soggily to his feet and started towards the blank tract of moor where last he had seen Sutton. A pace in front of him the heather trembled, water and turf spouted from the ponds between the heather. He sighted Sutton, further off than he had expected and prone, lifting his head from water, gesticulating in his direction.

What was the lad playing at? The guns banged. Peckover squelched towards the sergeant, holding his hat on his head with a peaty hand. His side hurt and a bead of rain which stung like a hailstone struck his chin.

But it was neither rain nor hail, he realized, and the realization brought him to a halt, feet sinking in puddles.

He was being shot at.

Whether boozily or with sober aim, Peckover did not wait to enquire. He threw himself flat. In peat of the consistency of chocolate mousse he lay like a fallen soldier. His raincoat he had left with his case in the police car, his hat had rolled into a miniature lake between the heather clumps. Much good were either here at Verdun, the guns thudding and no shell-craters to dive for. He needed a steel helmet. He reached for his hat.

'Sir!' rang out the sergeant's voice.

Peckover lifted his head. The grouse had gone and as abruptly as the bombardment had begun the guns of the western front had fallen silent. There was neither sight of life nor sound apart from two bounding, barking dogs which were not, he was relieved to see, heading in his direction. Again he failed to spot Sutton.

'Sergeant!' he shouted.

From the butts a twelve-bore boomed twice. Then another twelve-bore. Peckover lay flat. The guns roared. Sutton's been hit, he thought, prone in turf bog. Twisting his head, he saw a new squadron of grouse racing across the sky. He twisted further about. Beyond the police cars the infantry of beaters were still matchstick men dotting the moor. Twisting the other way, he saw the parked Land-Rovers and grouse-shoot cars. Their number had been swelled by one cream-coloured car.

The guns banged a blitzkrieg of shot and sound. Peckover levered himself higher. He had no need for binoculars to identify the cream car. Even as he looked the Cadillac started to move along the road in the direction of the police convoy. Behind, like an inebriate with confetti for a honeymoon couple, chased someone in white.

The figure ran hard, leaning forward with outstretched arm as though trying to catch hold of the fender. The Cadillac slid faster along the road leaving the figure standing, forlorn and white against the black moor.

The guns once more had fallen silent, the sky was bare. Peckover watched the Cadillac gather speed past the police cars, diminish to pinbox size and finally disappear over a crest in the road. For all he had been able to recognize of the driver at the wheel he might not have been Big Jack, he might have been the Home Secretary or the King of Siam. The figure in white was running back along the road towards the grouse-shoot cars. The two police cars had started to reverse over the heather. One behind the other they lurched back on to the road and accelerated after the Cadillac.

That's Zadiq there, get Zadiq, Peckover wanted to bawl after the fatuous police cars. He found that he was on his feet and running through heather towards the grouse-shoot cars, racing to reach them before Zadiq could reach them and flee; flee the moors and likely by this stage of the game, in some private jet, flee the country.

Peckover careered across the moor. No guns banged behind him from the butts. His slapping, squelching feet threw mud and water into his face. The police cars had vanished over the crest. Not a policeman in sight anywhere. Only himself and running Zadiq.

Where in hell was Sutton, what was the idiot up to? Peckover galloped grunting through bog. Miles still to go. Minutes anyway. Seconds if he were not swallowed by swamp. Did grouse-shooters lock their cars or leave them open? Already Zadiq had disappeared behind a Land-Rover.

He appeared again, white against the green Rover, bending and climbing in, then climbing out again and running to the BMW. Peckover bicycled his legs. His heart thumped, water sprayed over him. One foot sank up to the calf in swamp and he fell forward on hands and knees.

Why bother? Peckover asked himself. What did it matter if Zadiq fled the country? He was not here for

Zadiq, he was here for Olive Farnsworth.

So too were Crook and his men and they had her picture, Peckover remembered. They had no picture of Big Jack. Probably had never heard of Big Jack. And why would Big Jack abandon his sheikh and paymaster on this forsaken moor?

Peckover pounded on through the heather. So driving the Cadillac must have been Olive Farnsworth. And why not? She had not run to Ames-Clegg, she had run to Zadiq. If anyone had the loot to ship her from the country and set her up with a boutique in Brazil, Zadiq had. The only explanation for them arriving here was the settling of the hash for once and all of a snooping fraud inspector before reports were written and too much became general knowledge. Maybe Zadiq had wanted her along to keep her from getting gabby with other policemen. Maybe she had insisted on staying where the travel money was and seeing for herself the fraud policeman's hash settled.

Two fraud policemen. Both Sutton and himself had heard it all from Olive Farnsworth. Zadiq might have telephoned Ames-Clegg with an offer of a few thousand or million if both could be accidentally shot dead should they happen to show up for a grouse-shoot.

What did any of that matter either? Peckover's sodden shoes slapped on the road, past the Land-Rover. Ahead a glimpse of white vanished behind the BMW. Peckover swerved between a Mini and a station wagon. A dozen paces ahead Zadiq stood watching him through dark glasses, holding his handbag; then he ducked from sight between cars.

Peckover listened and watched. He heard and saw nothing. He trod on tiptoe along the side of the station wagon.

The whereabouts of Big Jack was something else that did not matter so long as he was not within fifty miles.

Peckover saw the white and ran. Zadiq was half way

through the front passenger door of the Silver Shadow.

'Get in then if you're goin',' Peckover said, and he pushed the white suit with such vigour that Zadiq was thrust across the seats. He landed crookedly against the far door, his dark glasses falling forward on his nose.

Peckover slammed the passenger door behind him, took the keys from the ignition and with his other hand gathered the white lapels in his fist. He jerked Zadiq into a sitting position.

'She ditch you, Sunshine? That 'er in your Cadillac?'

'You are hurting – '

'I said that 'er in your car? Mrs Farnsworth?'

'She will be sorry. She – '

'Where's Jack?'

'Jack? Who is Jack? Please let – '

'Your chauffeur, mate!'

'I don't know!'

'Is 'e with Mrs Farnsworth?'

'No!' Zadiq was trying to do too many things: wrest the peaty hands from his lapels, push his glasses back up his nose, recover the handbag from the floor. He gave up and let his hands flop. 'Listen, Peckover, I can make this easy for you – '

'Did 'e drive you up 'ere – your chauffeur?'

'Yes!'

'Then where is 'e?'

'I do not know! Truly. Somewhere. I do not know what is happening. Let me make it easy – '

'So where's Mrs Farnsworth gone? Why's she nicked your car?'

'How would I know? Panic? So many police. She did not expect so many police. Drive me to the airport, Peckover. You will live well for the rest – '

'Shut your face. Come up for the kill, 'ave you?'

'Listen – '

'You listen. Trying to avoid arrest, obstructing a police

officer. That's starters, cock. Conspiracy to murder is something else.' Bunching the lapels, Peckover lifted Zadiq from the seat, then dropped him back against the door. Where his hand had been the white suit was smeared with mud. 'That's on top of attempting to bribe a police officer. Bribing a Member of Parliament, bribing local government officials, those'll be separate charges. Likely a dozen separate charges unless you want to plead guilty, when they might be lumped together. Concealment of evidence in the case of Ann Evans, accessory to the murder of Malcolm York. Reckon fifteen years at least. Turn Queen's evidence on Jack, Mrs Farnsworth, Ames-Clegg, all your Greenmead cronies, you might get it reduced to ten. Or 'ave your counsel plead insanity.'

Zadiq was scrabbling on the floor for his handbag.

'Forget it,' Peckover said. He caught sight of himself in the driving mirror. Under the sodden hat he looked like Al Jolson. On his chin a bubble of dried blood stood out above the mud.

'We will do a deal,' Zadiq said.

'I almost feel sorry for you. You don't stand a monkey's. Plead insanity, you'll be detained at 'Er Majesty's pleasure somewhere like Broadmoor which won't be all that luxurious. They'll take away that bag for a start.' Peckover snatched the handbag from Zadiq, wound down the window and skimmed the handbag into the road. 'God knows why I'm telling you this but you get to some nutbin like Broadmoor, grease a few palms, you might be out in a couple of years. You'll be deported, you'll never see the White Cliffs again, every immigration officer in the country is going to 'ave your picture in 'is pocket. Still, better than being locked up. Pity you didn't clear out this morning, collect your cashmere and piss off.'

Through the opened window, across the road and on the moor, the infantry of beaters were no longer matchstickmen but a line of beef-fed farmers, labourers and hired

locals spaced out over a quarter of a mile. They advanced
in mackintoshes and wellington boots, thrashing with
sticks at the heather. The beater at each extremity of the
line and in the line's centre carried not only a stick but a
flag. In spite of the flags, the line was here and there
ragged. A stone's throw from the Silver Shadow one
booted schoolboy in an anorak was already crossing the
road. Others were still deep on the moor. Even as Peckover watched, two grouse soared from close by the en-
quiring stick of an elderly beater. The policeman turned
his head and looked the other way across the moor,
towards the butts. Nothing was to be seen, only the distant
protuberances of the butts like boils on the face of the
moor; then the winging pair of grouse, and in Peckover's
ears the boom of fresh volleys from the shotguns.

Boozy shooting, he judged. The grouse lifted up and on,
unscathed.

What the devil was up with Terry Sutton? Where was
the lad?

'You wait 'ere,' Peckover muttered, and he heard the
clink of dropped car keys as he clambered from the
Silver Shadow.

Walking, running, walking again, Peckover splashed
back in the direction of the butts. He glanced over his
shoulder towards the road in an endeavour to find his
bearings but with the police cars gone he had nothing on
which to take a bearing. He was no longer certain which
of the butts he and Sutton had headed for. In a straggling
line the beaters were crossing the road, some in advance,
others still probing and flailing the moor beyond the
road.

Peckover veered east at forty-five degrees towards the
two faraway protuberances which he hoped were the butts
he and the sergeant had headed for twenty minutes
earlier. As he ran, walked and again ran, stumbling and
muttering oaths, he looked for Sutton. His eyes swivelled

across the panorama of moor from east to west and
scouring the blank, black heather. He had lost Oliv
Farnsworth. All he needed was to lose his sergeant.

Rain started to fall. The sky was ashen, empty except for
rain. The butts were silent. Panting, Peckover blundered
on, wiping rain and sweat from his eyes.

'Sergeant!' he called.

Only his own squelching feet answered.

Still he refused to permit into what remained of his
brains the thought he knew to be clamouring for entry:
that Sutton was dead or dying, profusely and irremediably
bleeding to death by a hundred pellets from the grouse-
gun of Ames-Clegg. A second thought he dared not entertain was how far he would go if ever his hands circled the
neck of Ames-Clegg. He jumped like a dray-horse in an
attempt to clear a dank moat and came down with a
splash which sent up water as though from a depth-charge,
deluging him to his ears. He stumbled on through lumpy
heather.

'Sergeant!' he shouted. 'Terry lad! Where are you?'

'Sir!'

Peckover stopped dead. He could see no one.

'Sergeant? Hello?'

'Sir!'

'Don't bloody keep shouting "sir"!' Peckover bawled.
'Where the 'ell are you?'

No reply.

God, he's sulking, Peckover thought, lifting his face to
the rain and the grey heaven.

'Terry?' Peckover called in a soothing voice.

'Here, sir, to your left. I mean right. Sorry.'

Left, right, sorry – God above, was the lad dying or
trying it on? Slopping to his right, Peckover missed his
footing on a ridge and skidded down an incline into a
shallow hollow filled with abundant heather, water and
Sergeant Sutton.

n said. 'What've you been doing –

an, what've I been doing? Looking for
…een doing.'

…ust that, sorry, well, it's the mud.'

…grimaced through his minstrel's mudpack.
Sutt… himself spattered but around the flecks of dirt
his complexion was pale. He lay on his back on the
further incline of the hollow, one knee bent, the other at
an angle in the heather. He lifted himself on his elbows.

'Sorry,' Sutton said.

'Are you hit?'

'No, sir. I think my leg's broken. I fell in this sodding
hole.' His hand moved and rested on the leg angled in the
heather. 'Sorry, sir.'

Peckover swore. One shell-crater on the entire benighted moor and Sutton had to break his leg in it. He
paddled through the crater and bent to peer at the
trousered leg.

Sutton said, 'I saw Mr Crook and his lot drive off after
a flashy cream car, sir. And you running about. There's
a fair view from here. What's happening?'

'A grouse-shoot, lad. Grouse-shooting's 'appening. It's
a country sport for the quality.'

For the moment no grouse were being shot. All was
peaceful apart from the pattering rain. Peckover turned
his head and looked at Sutton's view. Fifty yards distant
advanced the booted beaters, slashing with their sticks
but discovering no grouse. Still in the vanguard, closest
to the policeman's crater, was the schoolboy in the anorak.
The flag-holders at the extremities of the line remained
matchstick-men a hundred yards away. Beyond the beaters
the Silver Shadow parted from the parked cars and Land-
Rovers and gathered speed along the road.

'That's Ames-Clegg's Rolls, sir – I think.'

Peckover watched the Silver Shadow accelerate in the

opposite direction from that taken by Olive Farnsworth
and the police. Glasgow direction? he wondered. Carlisle?
Did Carlisle have an airport?

'Was it Mrs Farnsworth in the flashy cream job, sir?'

'Yes.' Peckover turned back to the sergeant. 'You'll 'ave
to 'ang on till we get some 'elp. I can't shift you.'

'The blokes with the sticks are coming, sir.

'They're not blokes, they're beaters, get your termin-
ology right.' Peckover observed the angled leg without
touching it. A couple of beaters might be persuaded to
drop out, he supposed, and help chair-lift the sergeant to
the road. 'I'd sooner 'ang on for Crook and an ambulance.'

'I mean, there's the big one coming, sir, coming our
way – look. Do we know him?'

Peckover turned and looked.

'You don't, I do,' he said.

Big Jack in raincoat and chauffeur's cap had broken
from a position somewhere near the flag-bearer on the far
left, or he had come into and through the line from
behind. He was advancing at a steady pace in the policemen's direction.

'And 'e knows me.'

Peckover stood upright in the watery hollow. The flag-
bearer on the extreme left shouted at Big Jack and waved
his flag. Big Jack started to run. He was the length of a
football field away, bearing towards the Scotland Yard
men like a grotesque outsize full-back. Sutton hoisted
himself higher on his elbows.

'Who – ?'

'Keep your 'ead down. You'll be all right.'

Peckover hoped so. He climbed to the ridge of the
crater. There was no time for surveys, compasses and
stop-watches. Best hope for them both, he believed, would
be for himself to run fast at a right-angle from Big Jack,
drawing Big Jack after him, away from the fraud squad
crater and back through the beaters to the road and

grouse-shoot cars. What happened at the cars could be worried about when and if he arrived. Sooner or later Crook and his lads would be back.

Big Jack was making brisk progress. He carried a beater's stick like a knobkerrie which in the moment of truth would be discarded, Peckover suspected, for the switchblade.

Half a football pitch.

'Where're you going? Sir – '

Peckover had already gone, legs circling and splashing, hand clamping his hat to his head, galloping at a tangent away from Big Jack and towards the remote flag-bearer to the right. Ahead the beaters had stopped beating and stood in wonderment.

Could they be relied on for assistance? Peckover, gasping as he ran, dared not risk it. He was not in uniform, by the time he had identified himself Big Jack would have descended and who in his right mind was going to tackle Big Jack? Looking sideways, he saw that part one of the plan had succeeded. Big Jack's target was himself. The chauffeur had changed course and was aiming his full-back bulk towards a point, Peckover believed, between his policeman's shoulder-blades.

Part two of the plan was a flop. Not a hope he would reach the cars before Big Jack cut him off. Cut him off and cut him down.

Peckover swerved right, away from the beaters and the road beyond and towards heather wilderness and a horizon of switchbacking Cheviots. He looked back at Jack veering right, charging in his wake. Peckover swerved further right towards the only remaining haven. The butts which from the road had appeared as beehive blobs across the moor were clearly now, at fifty paces, squares of low inhabited wall. Two heads showed above the wall of the closest butt.

Peckover raced as though from a rabid rhino. Peat like

paste clogged his feet. Looking over his shoulder, he saw the rockface chauffeur dragging a leg out of swamp. Even as he looked the leg sucked free and Jack spurted forward. Peckover ran as he had never run. His hat had gone. Through his gasping and moaning he heard the chauffeur's shoes pounding a counterpoint with his own. In front a gun exploded and his face seemed to catch alight.

Guns ahead, Jack behind. Peckover flung himself flat as the gun banged again.

Peckover and the moor embraced one another. Why not this surprising moor for the end of it all? The moor was warm as the womb. Through the darkness passed Miriam, buxom and smiling. He tasted peat. He rolled over and lifted his head. No grouse were in the sky. Twenty yards away Big Jack lumbered towards him.

Fifteen yards. Big Jack was hobbling, narrowing the gap at half speed. His balloon face was decorated with mud and without expression. He had lost his cap. He had either lost or jettisoned his knobkerrie and in his hand he carried the switchblade. He trampled towards the policeman, a machine leaking oil but working more or less to order and too huge, too mindlessly dangerous to be stopped by anything less than – what was his name, the Aussie reporter? – twenty Irish bricklayers? He's been hit, Peckover thought, struggling up. Beyond Jack, beyond beaters in disarray, cars were slowing on the road.

Police? Tea and cakes for the grouse-shoot? Whoever they were they were too late. Peckover turned from Jack and stumbled on. From the butt close in front was fleeing a stout gentleman dressed in waterproof cape and sou'-wester like a herring fisherman. The head and shoulders inside the butt wore merrily chequered tweeds and a deerstalker.

He's lost his loader, Peckover thought, blundering through rain and mire. He has to do his own reloading. Poor man. Then he kills me. Bag for the day two hundred grouse, one policeman.

He could hear the rasping of the machine at his back.
Planks like a fence encased the peat butt a dozen strides
ahead, shoring it up against Northumbrian rain. Ames-
Clegg in the butt was fumbling with a twelve-bore.
Timing, it's all timing, it's too late, Peckover thought,
charging as the gun swung towards him. Sir Cyril Ames-
Clegg, I am arresting you on a number of charges, he
wanted to say. On a number of charges I shall enumerate
you will now accompany me to the police station no but
you may telephone there I must caution you that anything.

Peckover stared into the black circles of the twelve-
bore. He hurled himself forward and down as sheet light-
ning roared, rocking the universe. He remembered St
Anne's Court when someone had simply switched out the
lights.

CHAPTER XV

'Easy now.'

'Should I try and move transport up, sir?'

'Easy. Can you hear me?'

'He's a sight all right.'

'Don't stand there, Stokoe. Gather the guns. Find out
about that bloody ambulance.'

'Touch and go – what? I brought him down, the big
fella. You see it? You chaps see it? My goodness, another
moment. Touch and go, eh?'

Why couldn't they all belt up? His head hammered.
He had been here before, hadn't he? Though this was not
Vine Street. The air was pure and the voices were not
cockney but Geordie. The last voice had been a horse-
voice, neither cockney nor Geordie but plummy and

protesting and edged with hysteria. The lights came on, illumining Superintendent Crook in his raffish beret. The sky was patchily blue. Somewhere close by someone was panting like a dog.

'You see it?' Ames-Clegg demanded. 'My word, I saved your man's bacon. What kept you chaps? The big fella – '

'Get him out of it!' Crook cried, the beret swirling round.

Peckover turned his head towards the panting. A black setter with pink tongue sat in the heather an arm's length away, observing him. Ames-Clegg was protesting and struggling, his tweeded arms held by two constables.

'Sutton – Sergeant Sutton,' Peckover said.

'He's all right.'

'His leg's broken.'

'He'll be all right, we're shifting him now. There's an ambulance coming.'

Assisted by Crook and a uniformed sergeant, Peckover levered himself up against the wall of the butt. Inside his skull a navvy with a drill was drilling his way out. He assumed he had hit the fence, the wooden plank. His luck. He could see milling police and beaters, a herring fisherman in cape and sou'wester, and soaring into the mottled sky a troupe of grouse. No grouse-guns banged. Was it over for the day, prematurely, the grouse-shoot? He watched Ames-Clegg being pushed and pulled through the heather by the two constables.

'Just let him try and plead his parliamentary privilege out of this lot,' Crook said. Crouched beside the Scotland Yard inspector, he too watched the struggling Ames-Clegg. 'You've a bottle of champagne coming, Peckover. And we've got the Farnsworth woman. Want to see her?'

'No.'

'She keeps jabbering about this Zadiq. Is he here?'

''E was. I've got to phone the Yard. 'E ought to get away.'

'Get away?'

'Out of it. We've nothing on 'im, nothing worthwhile.' Peckover reached out and gripped the plank which encased the butt. 'Simplest for everyone. Got to phone the commissioner.'

'Easy, chum. Can you stand?'

Peckover found that he could. His skull sang and he believed that an earlier pellet or two from the twelve-bore of Ames-Clegg might be lodged in his face and side. But he could stand. Supported by worried Crook and the sergeant, he could even put one waterlogged shoe in front of the other.

'Who was he, then?' Crook said, inclining his head towards the prostrate and pellet-riddled heap of mud, raincoat and tan leggings in the heather.

'Jack,' Peckover said.

The commissioner hummed, hawed and did a fair amount of throat-clearing. Simpler or not, he argued, allowing a villain like Zadiq to flee the country was the feeble way out, contrary to law and morality. What future was there for impartial justice if every suspected criminal were allowed willy-nilly to flash his passport and hop the first flight out of Heathrow?

When by the following evening no word of Zadiq's detention had reached Detective-Inspector Peckover in his hospital bed, either by newspaper, radio or his stream of visitors, he knew that the commissioner had plumped for simplicity and feebleness.

By the Friday afternoon Peckover was up and travelling west along the M4 in the front passenger seat of his Cortina. Bandages enveloped not only his head but his cheeks and chin, lending him a resemblance to a knight dressed for a joust. More bandages bound his torso,

swelling the bulk beneath the holiday shirt and aged
sports jacket. A string of hospital appointments reached
ahead of him. Even more tiresome was the Ames-Clegg
£500, still in Terry Sutton's desk.

Easiest of all would be to shut up about it. Halve it
down the middle, or for that matter give the sergeant the
lot, something to celebrate with once his leg was mended.
But he'd have to be careful, watch the sergeant's eyes when
he mentioned it. No point tempting a promising lad off the
straight and narrow.

Untidy, messy. Give yourself a couple of weeks or a
month, the commissioner had said. As long as necessary.

Then back to it. The Mountains. Beeston still in the
Algarve. The day he got back to the fraud office he'd be
opening Molehill part seven. For a fraught moment he
had believed the commissioner was going to ask if he were
interested in promotion to Co-ordinator (Metropolitan
Area), Community Relations.

He reflected that none of the capering of the last couple
of months would have happened but for Ann Evans. But
for Olive Farnsworth killing her. It had all started from
Ann Evans. Unless of course you went right back to greed,
good old twentieth-century materialism. Adam and Eve.

'Right at the crossroads,' he said.

'I know, I know,' Miriam said. 'You know I don't want
to meet him. If he's there I'm staying in the car.'

'Me too,' murmured Peckover.

There was no car on the grass verge outside the cottage.
If the DC were in residence he was for the moment off
somewhere, probably with his shyster lawyer. Peckover
led past the back door to the shed and opened the door.
He dug through the earth in the third seedlings tray and
pulled out a wedge of *Evening Standard*. He shook off the
soil, unfolded the newspaper and looked in at a wad of
twenties.

Miriam said, 'What's that?'

'My price,' Peckover said. 'He was spot on.'

'But you can't. It's from that Zadiq, isn't it?'

'That's right.'

'I mean you can't. They'll know – they must know.'

'Who knows? Zadiq knows. 'E's not going to say anything.'

Peckover tucked the *Evening Standard* and twelve thousand pounds into his inside pocket. He bent down and brushed the soil back in place.

'But you can't keep it!'

'Who's keeping it? It'll be spent by next week. The rates, that thin bit on the roof, a dirty weekend in Bournemouth, the two of us.' He closed the shed door behind her and sniffed the country garden. 'Anyway, who's talking? Who brings 'ome a couple of kilos of the archaeologists' moussaka every evening?'

He walked back along the path. Miriam scurried after.

'That's different. I mean – twelve thousand! You're not like that! You're – you're a poet!'

'Right, love. So shut up and drive. I've got a poem coming on.'